W9-AAC-713

**"Where are you going?"**

Jaycee grabbed Brett's arm, panic filling her face.

"I'm going to get our horse and we're getting out of here. We can't stay pinned down." The horse was a bigger target for the sniper to hit but they could get out of range faster on it than on foot. He had to risk it.

He climbed to his feet and headed into the field, shielding his movement with the horse's body as best he could until he reached it. Once he did, he quickly climbed into the saddle and headed toward Jaycee.

Gunfire erupted from the sniper but Brett moved quickly. He urged the horse into the brush where Jaycee hid, then lifted her up behind him.

Just as she settled in, shots fired again. The horse startled and she nearly slid as he bucked. Brett held on to the reins as Jaycee clung to his jacket.

"Get out of here!" she cried and Brett wasted no time.

He spun the horse around and took off.

Their safe, protective hideout had been breached.

**Virginia Vaughan** is a born-and-raised Mississippi girl. She is blessed to come from a large Southern family, and her fondest memories include listening to stories recounted around the dinner table. She was a lover of books from a young age, devouring tales of romance, danger and love. She soon started writing them herself. You can connect with Virginia through her website, virginiavaughanonline.com, or through the publisher.

## Books by Virginia Vaughan

### Love Inspired Suspense

***Cowboy Protectors***

*Kidnapped in Texas*
*Texas Ranch Target*

***Cowboy Lawmen***

*Texas Twin Abduction*
*Texas Holiday Hideout*
*Texas Target Standoff*
*Texas Baby Cover-Up*
*Texas Killer Connection*
*Texas Buried Secrets*

***Covert Operatives***

*Cold Case Cover-Up*
*Deadly Christmas Duty*
*Risky Return*
*Killer Insight*

Visit the Author Profile page at LoveInspired.com for more titles.

# Texas Ranch Target

## Virginia Vaughan

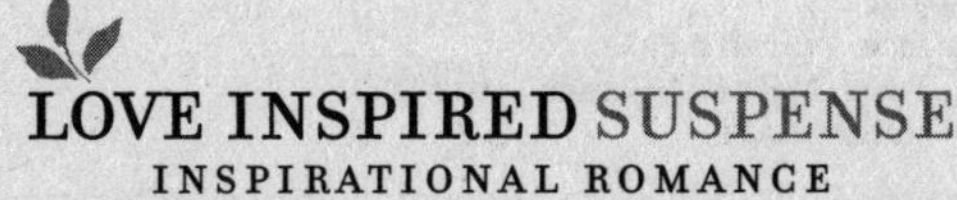

If you purchased this book without a cover you should be aware that this book is stolen property. It was reported as "unsold and destroyed" to the publisher, and neither the author nor the publisher has received any payment for this "stripped book."

Recycling programs for this product may not exist in your area.

ISBN-13: 978-1-335-58771-8

Texas Ranch Target

Copyright © 2023 by Virginia Vaughan

All rights reserved. No part of this book may be used or reproduced in any manner whatsoever without written permission except in the case of brief quotations embodied in critical articles and reviews.

This is a work of fiction. Names, characters, places and incidents are either the product of the author's imagination or are used fictitiously. Any resemblance to actual persons, living or dead, businesses, companies, events or locales is entirely coincidental.

For questions and comments about the quality of this book, please contact us at CustomerService@Harlequin.com.

Love Inspired
22 Adelaide St. West, 41st Floor
Toronto, Ontario M5H 4E3, Canada
www.LoveInspired.com

**Printed in U.S.A.**

And we know that all things work together for good
to them that love God, to them who are the called
according to his purpose.

—*Romans* 8:28

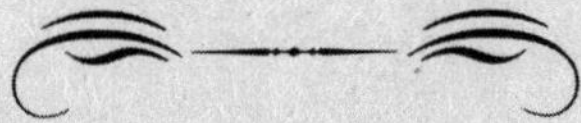

This book is dedicated to my readers
for your continued faithfulness and encouragement.

# ONE

Jaycee Richmond stared out the hotel window at the darkening skyline of small-town Jessup, Texas. Her phone dinged with another pop-up about last month's murder of actress Whitney Warren and the failure of security expert Brett Harmon to keep the celebrity safe.

The press was blaming Brett but Jaycee knew they didn't have the whole story.

Neither did Brett.

Jaycee had come to Jessup specifically to track him down. She had information about Whitney's murder that he needed to know.

Information that could change his life.

And end hers.

Someone had already tried to silence her, sending her fleeing from her home yesterday in a spray of gunfire to search out the security expert. Only, Brett had been keeping a low profile since Whitney's murder and the publicity surrounding it had all but shut down his security business. Probably only a handful of people knew he was heading here, and Jaycee was one of them. She'd had to use some creative ways of tracking him to his hometown, including tapping into his cell phone. She glanced at her computer screen and the GPS indicator that showed Brett was less than an hour away from arriving in Jessup.

*Hurry up, Brett. I have something important to tell you.*

She heard something and turned from the window. The doorknob on her hotel room door moved ever so slightly.

She gasped and reached for the gun she'd grabbed when the shooting at her apartment had started. She'd taken a class when she'd bought the gun for protection but had never fired it. Never had a reason to before now.

The man who'd already tried to kill her once had followed her to town.

She inched toward the door. She'd secured the main lock, which should prevent him from getting inside, yet she couldn't resist checking it again. He must have noticed her movement from beneath the door because seconds later the door burst open. Jaycee tumbled backward, hitting her head against the dresser as the gun slipped from her hand. Her attacker grabbed her. He shoved her to the floor and pressed one hand over her mouth, his other arm crushing against her throat, cutting off her air. She kicked and struggled against him, trying to breathe but unable to budge him.

Panic gripped her as her vision tunneled. If she lost consciousness, she was going to die and Brett would never know the truth.

Her attacker would get away with murder again.

She flailed her hands for something, anything, to

fight back with. One hand locked onto the lamp that had fallen to the floor during the struggle. She gripped it and swung it as hard as she could at the side of his head.

Her attacker loosened his hold and slumped to the side, unconscious.

Jaycee scrambled to her feet and ran from the room, hurrying down the stairwell before her attacker got up and followed her. Her heart raced as she burst into the lobby. No one was around and the front desk was unoccupied. Her gaze landed on the phone in the lobby. She had to call the police. She should have gone to them after he'd attacked her at her apartment but she'd wanted to come clean to Brett first about what she'd done.

Now, she had no choice. She headed for the table that held the phone. The elevator dinged, startling her, and she jumped and cried out. She spun around as the doors slid open. What if it was the man who'd attacked her?

She didn't have time to wait for the police. She had to get out of there now.

Jaycee stumbled toward the front entrance and pushed through the doors. Her head pounded and blood dripped into her face, but she didn't have time to catalog her injuries right now. She had to get as far away from her attacker as she could.

She hurried to her car, thankful the keys were still in her pocket. She started the engine and drove away. Her mirrors showed no signs of her attacker but that didn't mean he wasn't coming. He'd found her in Dallas and again here in Jessup. He wouldn't stop until he'd silenced her for good.

A sharp pain ripped through her head and her vision

blurred. The car drifted from the lane. She overcorrected the other way before bringing the vehicle under control. Thankfully, there were no other cars on the road.

Where was she even going? She didn't know.

Until she did.

Brett was on his way into town and she'd tracked his phone. He was coming in on the main highway. If she had to, she would meet him halfway. He had to know the truth about Whitney's death. He had to know it wasn't his fault.

She needed to clear her own guilty conscience.

Headlights glared in her rearview mirror as a vehicle fast approached behind her. Fear swamped her. It had to be her assailant. He wasn't finished with her.

She pressed the accelerator, speeding up. The vehicle kept coming. The pounding in her head intensified and her vision blurred again. Her head hurt so badly either from hitting the dresser or her attacker trying to cut off her air supply. She took a deep breath and did her best to push away the fuzz that was enveloping her mind.

She had to stay alert if she wanted to live.

She pressed the gas pedal again as the car pulled up behind her. It did no good. Her car was already going as fast as it would go. Her assailant's vehicle was just faster. She felt his eyes on her and dared to glance his way as he pulled up beside her. His smug grin told her all she needed to know. She wasn't going to make it out of this.

He jerked the wheel and rammed into her car, sending her vehicle spinning out of control. She screamed as it left the ground and flipped, again and again, finally stopping only when it bounced off the guardrail then skidded to a stop upside down.

Jaycee hit her head again and pain riddled through her. She blacked out but was certain it was only for a moment. When she came to, the other car had stopped and footfalls were hurrying toward her.

*Thump, thump. Thump, thump.*

The sound matched the pounding in her head.

Panic pushed her to unbuckle and crawl toward the shattered passenger's-side window despite the protests of her aching body. She couldn't give up now. She couldn't allow him to win.

Then, suddenly, the thumping footfalls stopped. She pushed herself out of the car in time to see her assailant hurry back to his vehicle and roar away in the direction he'd come.

What had happened?

She forced herself to her feet and stumbled into the road. Headlights rolled over her. She raised her hands to shield her eyes from the blinding light as tires squealed, the smell of rubber sickening her.

A car headed straight for her.

Brett Harmon slammed on his brakes as a woman appeared out of nowhere in the road. He jerked the steering wheel and crossed the yellow line. Thankfully, there was no oncoming traffic this time of evening and this far out of town. His Charger skidded to a stop.

Adrenaline rushed through him at the near miss.

He'd almost hit the woman.

Then came the relief and the anger at being put into that situation again.

Two deaths in a month's time?

He couldn't be responsible for another woman's death.

Brett threw the gear into Park then turned off the ignition and jumped out. He circled the car and headed toward the woman, stopping when he saw her. She was kneeling on the asphalt, her long blond hair disheveled. Both her hair and clothes were covered in blood from a gash on her head, but it was the look of confusion in her expression that really grabbed him.

He took a breath then noticed the vehicle on its roof and the smashed guardrail several feet away. From the looks of the car, she shouldn't have survived that crash.

He approached her cautiously. She didn't appear seriously injured but the confused look worried him. She could have suffered anything from a concussion to internal injuries. "Are you okay, miss?"

She didn't speak right away and in fact almost seemed like she hadn't heard him. However, as he took another step closer, she moved back from him. "Is there someone I can call for you?"

She raised her eyes to look at him then shook her head so very slightly. Suddenly all the angry heat and resentment he'd felt earlier washed away. His issues weren't her fault. She needed help.

"What's your name?"

She stared up at him, her eyes big and brown and round. Suddenly fear entered them along with confusion and panic.

"Do you know your name?"

She opened her mouth to speak. "I—yes, of course, I know my name. It's…it's…" She tilted her head, a clear indication she was trying to recall. Tears filled her eyes.

He knelt to her eye level. "My name is Brett Harmon. You look like you could use some help. What happened?"

Her face twisted, and she finally shook her head.

Brett pushed to his feet and held out his hand to her. "Why don't you let me take you to the hospital?"

Her hand shook as she extended it, but she trusted him enough to allow him to lead her to his car.

She slid into the front passenger seat. His protective instincts kicked in. Her car was damaged pretty good and she'd probably suffered a concussion. It wasn't unusual for deer to dart out into the road at night, making drivers swerve to miss them. That could be what had happened to her.

He walked around to the driver's side of the Charger and reached for his cell phone. This woman needed help and to get to safety. He could call the ambulance but it would take them a while to get out here. The best thing would be to drive her to the hospital, but he'd also need some help when he got there.

He dialed the number for the Jessup Police Department and asked for the chief of police. The receptionist didn't want to connect him until he informed her that the chief was his cousin and he had an emergency.

A few minutes later, Caleb came on the line. "Brett, what's going on? I haven't heard from you in a while."

"Hey, Caleb. We can catch up later, but right now

I have a real problem. I was heading into town and I nearly ran someone over."

His tone morphed into a more professional one immediately. "Was anyone hurt?"

"I didn't hit her but she obviously needs help. It looks like her car flipped multiple times. She's dazed but not seriously injured. The thing is, she can't remember her name. I'm taking her to the hospital now."

"I'll meet you there," Caleb stated.

Brett ended the call then slid his phone back into his pocket. He climbed into the driver's seat and closed the door. He looked at the woman shivering in the seat beside him. "Do you need help putting on your seat belt?"

She didn't speak, only looked at him like she didn't understand what he was talking about. Finally, he reached over, grabbed the seat belt and put it around her. She seemed surprised by his action but didn't stop him.

"I'm going to take you to the hospital. They'll be able to help you there. It's not uncommon to have some memory loss after a wreck. You probably hit your head." In fact, he was sure of it based on the gash still dripping blood down her face. He found some napkins in his console and pressed one against her forehead to stop the bleeding. "Hold this here until we get to the ER."

She took hold of the napkin as he'd asked but a single tear slid down her cheek, making a trail through the blood. She looked so fragile sitting in the passenger seat and he flashed back to Whitney lying on the floor in her hotel room, bleeding out in his arms, unable to speak. She'd trusted him to protect her and he'd failed her.

His firm had handled security for a lot of well-known

celebrities, but Whitney Warren's case had been different. She'd been engaged to a member of Brett's marine squad; only, Tony had never made it home from their last mission. When Whitney had found herself with an unknown stalker, she'd hired his firm primarily because of the connection to Tony.

Brett had personally handled her security and he'd been confident in his ability to keep her safe. But everything on that job had gone sideways. Someone had gotten through his security measures and managed to murder Whitney. She'd died because he hadn't been able to do his job sufficiently. Now his reputation, and his company's, had taken a hit. The company's rep was nothing compared to Whitney losing her life, but Brett was personally bearing all the blame for what had happened. And he wouldn't be able to rest until he found the person who'd killed her.

Now, he'd stumbled upon another woman who needed his assistance. Well, he was glad to give her a ride to the hospital then let the police handle it from there. He couldn't be responsible for anyone else at the moment. He started the engine and headed into town.

They arrived at the hospital and Brett parked by the emergency room doors. He called for help as he led the woman inside. Once he explained the situation, a nurse took over, escorting her behind a set of double doors. "You wait here," she commanded Brett, leaving him standing in the waiting area.

He didn't have to wait long before the hospital doors slid open and his cousin Caleb arrived. Another of his cousins, Luke, was with him. Luke, a former FBI agent who'd retired from the agency a few months ago, had resettled in Jessup on the ranch their grandfather had left them all a piece of.

Brett hadn't seen either of his cousins in over six years and had only spoken to them a handful of times since then, but it was good to see them now.

Caleb approached him first. "Where is she?"

"The nurse took her back a few minutes ago. She looked confused and couldn't tell me her name."

"Did you check to see if she had any identification on her?" Luke asked.

"I didn't," Brett stated. "She already looked so violated, I didn't want to risk searching her for that. She wasn't carrying a purse but it could have been in the car. You'll find what's left of it over on the main highway about five miles south of town."

Caleb nodded. "I'll send Luke and one of my officers to investigate."

Brett checked the GPS data on his cell phone then texted it to Luke. "That's the location."

Luke glanced at his phone and nodded, confirming he'd received the coordinates. "I'll call Hansen and we'll check out the area."

Brett waited for Luke to walk off before he turned to Caleb. "I knew Luke had retired from the FBI but I didn't realize he was working for you."

Caleb shrugged. "He doesn't really. We were together at the ranch when I received your call. Dispatch forwarded it to my cell phone. Luke decided to tag along. He helps out now and then when a case piques his interest, but he's mostly retired and spending time getting to know his daughter."

Brett had learned when he'd made plans to come to the ranch that Luke, upon his return to Jessup, had discovered his high school sweetheart had given birth to a child then given her to her sister to raise. She'd gotten custody back when her sister and brother-in-law had died in a car accident, but Luke hadn't discovered he'd had a fourteen-year-old daughter until she'd been abducted by a human trafficking ring.

"How are you doing?" Caleb asked him.

He wasn't surprised at the question. His cousins had known he was returning to Jessup and his nightmare failure had been front-page news for weeks now. Whitney's murder. Brett's failure as a security specialist. Everyone knew.

"I'm holding up," he said, lying through his teeth. He'd been hoping to hide out at Harmon Ranch until all the dust settled. He could never bring back Whitney, but if the police didn't find her killer soon, he was determined he would do whatever it took to find him and bring him to justice. He owed that to Whitney.

Knowing his cousin well enough to not believe his posturing, Caleb let it slide. "Let's go check on this woman you found."

Brett was grateful to have the distraction. Not that he was glad he'd nearly hit someone. That had scared him half to death. She'd come out of nowhere, although he couldn't deny he'd probably been a little bit distracted as notifications about Whitney's death and the police investigation had continued to pop up on his phone as "breaking news."

Caleb flashed his badge, although Brett was certain

he didn't need to. Jessup was a small town and everyone knew Caleb was the chief of police. A nurse led them back through double doors to a curtained-off area. The woman he'd found lay on the hospital bed. They'd cleaned her up and given her a gown to wear instead of the clothes he'd found her in. A bandage now covered the gash he'd pressed his console napkins to.

A doctor met them at the cubicle opening. "We've treated her injuries, Chief. She's got some cuts and bruises, perhaps from the wreck, as well as a gash on her forehead and a bump on the back of her head. Possibly a mild concussion, but no life-threatening injuries."

Caleb nodded. "That's good to hear."

"There's something else." The doctor pulled them both aside and lowered her voice. "There's bruising on her neck. Looks like strangulation marks to me. She doesn't remember what happened or how they got there."

"She's blocked out the attack?"

"She's done more than that. She can't even remember her own name much less what happened to her. Memory loss after an accident isn't uncommon, but it's usually limited to the events of the accident. Her memory is gone."

"Do you think it'll return?" Brett asked.

She shrugged. "That's difficult to know. The amnesia could be from the bumps on her head or trauma from the attack. We'll run some more tests, but I'd say the best thing we can do now is try to help her remember who she is."

Brett rubbed his head. "Only we don't know who

she is. Did she have any identification in her clothes? A wallet? A cell phone?"

"I'm not sure. We bagged everything when she came in. I'll send someone to get it."

"Can we speak with her?"

"We're taking her up for a CT scan in a few minutes."

"It'll be quick," Caleb assured her.

He stepped toward the bed and Brett followed him. Bruises on her face, arms and neck were evident under the harsh light. Brett hadn't noticed them earlier.

"My name is Caleb Harmon, ma'am. I'm the chief of police here in Jessup. You've already met my cousin, Brett Harmon. How are you doing?"

She sucked in a breath and Brett could see she was fighting to keep control. Her voice was raspy when she spoke. "Not so good."

"Can you tell me your name?"

That confusion Brett had seen earlier seeped back into her face.

She lowered her head and fiddled with her fingers. "I don't remember."

"Do you remember anything about what happened to you?"

"No. All I remember is waking up in the car and this indescribable feeling of having to get away. I had no idea where I was or what had happened. I still don't even know where I am."

"You're at Jessup Medical Center in Jessup, Texas."

An orderly brought in a plastic bag. Brett took it then thanked him. "Maybe there's something in your clothes that'll help you remember. Do you mind if we look?"

She nodded, giving him the okay.

He moved the bag to the bed and he and Caleb looked through it. Just as he'd thought, there was no purse or wallet, but she might be the type to keep her identification in her pocket. He pulled out her clothes and dug through her pants' pockets. He felt something in the back pocket.

"Feels like a business card."

Now they were getting somewhere. Wherever this card was from, maybe the business would remember her. He pulled it out and turned it over, stunned by the name on the card.

*Brett Harmon, Security Specialist, B&W Security.*

Brett sucked in a breath. What was his business card doing on the woman he'd nearly run down?

Caleb noticed it, too, and his jaw clenched. He pulled Brett aside. "Is she one of your clients?"

He shook his head. "I've never seen her before. I have no idea how she got one of my business cards. I only hand those cards out to my clients." However, given his recent scandal, there was no shortage of people trying to get in touch with him. "She could be a reporter looking to get a comment from me about the Whitney Warren fiasco."

Caleb nodded. "That might explain why she's in town but not why she was assaulted and crashed her car."

Brett had to agree. He walked over to the bed and held out the card to her. "This is my business card for my security firm. Do you have any idea how you got it?"

She took the card from him and looked at it, then shook her head and handed it back to him. "I don't know.

I don't even remember my name much less how I got your card."

Caleb's cell phone dinged and he pulled it out. "It's from Luke. They found the car."

"Is there identification inside?"

His cousin's shoulders slumped. "No. The registration from the vehicle says the owner's name is Russell Stewart." He looked at the woman. "Ring any bells? Is that your husband maybe?"

She glanced at her hand. "I don't know, but I'm not wearing a wedding ring."

Brett sighed. They were getting nowhere fast in figuring out who this woman was.

"I'm going to have one of my officers come to the hospital and take your fingerprints. If you're in the database somewhere, we'll figure out who you are. Then we'll figure out who tried to harm you."

She nodded her agreement and he placed the call.

Brett hoped she was in the system. They needed to put a name to this woman fast. He stared at the marks on her neck. He hadn't noticed those earlier but they indicated someone had attacked her. Had she been escaping from him as she'd crashed her car?

He didn't like the idea of someone he didn't know possessing one of his cards he reserved for clients. She had to have it for a reason. Was it because she'd been searching for him to get a story…or because she needed his help?

Her head ached and the tears threatened to burst through the edge of her lids as she was taken for the CT scan. She didn't want to break down in front of these strangers…but who did she know who wasn't a stranger? She was a stranger even to herself.

Caleb had left, but Brett was waiting for her when they took her to a private hospital room after the scan. He had said he was staying until the officer came to fingerprint her. He wanted to know her identity as much as she did and he kept questioning her about his business card in her pocket. She didn't know why it had been there. If she'd been seeking him out for something or if it was merely a coincidence, she couldn't say for certain.

No. That wasn't true.

She glanced at him and felt something familiar. His square jaw and light brown hair and sideburns stirred something inside her. She'd seen his face and was certain she'd been looking for him. But why? She didn't know the answers to that.

A woman with blond hair and a big smile appeared at the curtained opening. She stepped inside and reached her hand out to Brett. "Hi. I'm Abby Harmon, Luke's wife."

She had no idea who Luke was, but Brett seemed to understand, responding with, "It's nice to meet you, Abby. I've heard a lot about you."

She laughed nervously. "I'm not sure if I should take that as a good thing or not." Abby's face softened as she turned to look at her. "Caleb asked me to come by. I'm a reporter for the local TV station. He thought if we did a story on you, someone might come forward to help identify you. Would you mind that?"

She sat up in bed. She didn't know what to say. She

looked horrendous and vanity was her first response. She pushed that away and nodded her agreement. "If this will help figure out who I am, I'm willing."

The woman pulled up a chair to the bedside and littered her with questions. She answered all of them the best she could, but that wasn't many. Abby was kind and gentle and she liked her instantly.

"I think I have everything I need except a picture," Abby said, standing. She pulled out her cell phone, opened the camera app and aimed it at her. The camera clicked as she snapped the picture. "We'll run this on the ten o'clock news tonight. Hopefully, it will provide some answers for you."

Abby glanced once again at Brett. "It was nice to meet you. I'll probably see you back at the ranch. I'm not sure if you know but we're living there now too."

He nodded and watched her walk out.

"Apparently, she just married my cousin Luke. He, Caleb, my other cousin Tucker and I just inherited our grandfather's ranch. I haven't even been back in Jessup in years."

"She seemed nice. I hope something helps. I'm so tired of not being able to remember things." It was exhausting trying to pull information from her head and getting blocked at every turn. It was as if a wall had been erected between her and her memories. She blew out a frustrated sigh. "Why can't I remember?"

"You were hit on the head. It could be a medical reason. We'll have to wait on the CT results. Or it could be the trauma you've endured. The attack then the car crash is enough to make anyone not want to remember."

"But I do want to remember. I want to know who did this to me and why."

He nodded and took her hand, the touch of which sent electricity zinging up her arm. She sucked in a breath to keep herself from reacting. *What was that about?* "So do I," she said trying to keep her voice steady so he wouldn't notice how his simple touch had affected her.

Brett showed no signs of a reaction to that spark, leaving her to speculate he must not have felt anything. Great. She was falling all over herself over a guy whose only concern about her was that she'd been carrying his business card when she was attacked. "Is it possible I picked up your card at a business? Some restaurants have those places where you can leave your card as an advertisement for others to find."

Now why did she remember that but not her own name?

He shook his head.

"I only hand those out to clients. For other functions, we have company business cards we use. If you had one of those, I might not think anything about it, but you have my personal business card. It has my private number on it. Only clients get those. It's possible you got it from one of my clients. Someone obviously set out to hurt you. Maybe you were trying to hire me and a former client gave it to you." He shrugged and rubbed his chiseled chin. "I'm grasping at straws here."

She sighed at the disappointment in his face. They both wanted answers. "I wish I could remember."

An officer stopped by to take her fingerprints. Then, at 10:00 p.m., Brett turned on the TV to the local news.

The woman she'd met earlier—Abby—was sitting at the anchor desk. She looked as beautiful as she had when she'd stopped by and she understood why Abby was on TV.

Abby detailed the story of her being found after the car crash and her amnesia, then showed her photo on screen. She flinched at the image. She looked terrible with no makeup and bruises and bandages on her face. But she couldn't focus on her appearance. Someone watching this broadcast might know her and come forward to identify her. Then she would finally get some answers.

Abby finished up the story by asking that anyone with information about her identity contact the local police department.

"That should help us figure this out," Brett stated as he clicked off the TV. "But I'm going to alert security to your room. If whoever attacked you saw that broadcast then he knows you survived. He might try again."

Goose bumps raised on her skin at the thought that whoever had tried to hurt her might try again. She hadn't even considered that possibility.

"Don't worry," Brett said when he saw her reaction. "You're safe here tonight. There'll be a guard on your door and I'll check back in on you tomorrow. Maybe by then Caleb will have run your fingerprints and discovered your name and identity."

She was hopeful that would be the case. The best scenario was that she just remembered everything. That seemed unlikely though the doctor had said her memories could come flooding back to her at any moment.

Or never at all.

Brett said good-night then walked out.

She slid down into the bed and tried to sleep but her mind was racing with questions that held no answers. And she kept spiraling to the one thing she knew for certain: someone had tried to kill her tonight.

She finally fell into a light sleep but was awakened in the early morning hours by the door opening. Light filtered into the darkened room. She assumed it was another nurse coming to check on her. There had been two already before she fell asleep. One to check her vitals and another to bring her a tray with something to eat. She turned in the bed to speak but was startled by the figure standing over her bed. The light from behind cast a shadow over him and she couldn't see his face, but everything about his posture and stance screamed that he was wrong. He didn't belong there.

She opened her mouth to call out but he yanked the pillow from behind her head and covered her face before she could, pressing down hard. She pulled at the pillow, trying to push it away as the sensation of not being able to breathe grabbed hold. Panic filled her. She clawed at his hands and arms and kicked her legs, doing everything in her power to shove him away, but he was too strong and easily overpowered her.

Her hand felt for a knife on the food tray on the table by the bed. She couldn't see the man but she knew if she could hit a vulnerable spot, he might loosen his grip. She stabbed at him and heard him grunt in pain, but his grasp didn't weaken. Finally, she jabbed the knife hard and felt it dig into his flesh. He cried out and his weighty hold lessened.

She fell from the bed, gasping for air as she saw the man stumble backward. She had to act quickly before he regained his composure and came at her again.

She crawled under the bed and grabbed the cord to ring for the nurse, knowing she wouldn't arrive in time and, if she did, he might lash out at her too. She had no choice. She had to call for help.

He circled the bed and grabbed her feet, pulling her toward him. Her head was spinning from the concussion and attempted suffocation, but she wasn't going down without a fight.

She spun around and dug the butt of her hand into his face, hitting him in the neck and causing him to gasp. Instinctively, she scrambled to her feet and turned to run, pulling open the hospital door and darting into the hallway. He grabbed her and dragged her back inside. She kicked up a commotion, overturning everything she could as he pulled her to the floor and pressed his hands into her neck.

He was wearing a mask, so even though they were face-to-face, she couldn't see what he looked like except for dark, angry eyes.

Footsteps and shouts down the hall indicated the commotion had been detected. Her attacker must have heard it, too, because he let her go and darted from the room just minutes before a nurse and a security guard rushed inside.

She pushed herself to a sitting position, holding her neck as pain radiated from it. Every breath she took hurt, but she was thankful for it, remembering the suffocating feeling of the pillow being held over her face.

"Honey, are you okay?" The nurse helped her into bed. Meanwhile, the security guard had called in an intruder alert and was now peppering her with questions about what her attacker looked like.

She wasn't much help in that regard. She couldn't describe him.

She lay back on the bed and struggled to breathe as one thought rushed through her.

He'd tried to kill her…again.

Someone wanted her dead and, thanks to her lack of memory, she had no idea why.

# TWO

Brett awoke before dawn and stared around his old bedroom, the one he'd used whenever he'd come to stay at Harmon Ranch as a child. The house had enough bedrooms that Brett's grandfather had been able to give each of his four grandsons their own space for whenever they visited. The last time he'd been in this room, he'd been sixteen, and yet it was still decorated for a teenaged boy, with model airplanes and posters of fast cars hanging on the wall. He was used to waking in strange hotel rooms or safe houses due to his security work, but waking in this old bedroom and being blasted by the past was surreal.

How had he ended up back here?

He picked up his phone to check his messages and saw several pop-up notifications about Whitney Warren.

Oh yeah. That was how.

He should turn the notifications off but he couldn't bring himself to do so. He owed a debt to Whitney and reading those notifications seemed like a means of atonement.

He showered and dressed then found his cousins, Abby, and a teenage boy and girl in the kitchen seated around a large, round table.

Luke stood and made introductions. "Brett, this is my wife, Abby."

Brett nodded. "We met yesterday at the hospital."

"And these are our kids, Kenzie and Dustin."

"Nice to meet you," Brett said.

Luke looked happy. He had his ready-made family and it seemed everything had worked out okay for everyone involved.

Brett was happy for him, but it wasn't what he was looking for. He'd spent his life since leaving the marines traveling and working high-security jobs, enjoying the celebrity and fame that went along with delivering private protection services. Some media outlets had snapped photos of him and even speculated that he and Whitney had been an item. It was entirely false. Whitney had been faithful to the memory of her fiancé, Tony Davenport, another US Marine who'd been killed in combat. Besides, Brett didn't date the people he'd promised to protect.

Caleb's phone buzzed and he reached to answer it. His face turned grim as he listened to the caller on the other end. "Okay. Send a team there to collect evidence. I'm on my way." He ended the call and slid his phone back into its holster on his belt. "There was an incident at the hospital," he said. "We'd better get down there."

The worry on Caleb's face sent Brett's pulse rising. "Is she okay?"

"Someone knocked the security guard out that was

guarding her door, slipped into her room and attacked her. She managed to get away, but the head of security said they nearly didn't make it there in time."

"Did they capture the assailant?" Luke asked.

He shook his head. "He got away. I'll coordinate with the security team to get video surveillance once we arrive. Brett, you'd better go check on your lady friend and make certain she's okay."

He nodded and hurried back upstairs to grab his jacket, gun and phone. His heart was racing and he grimaced. He should have remained with her, but she wasn't his client. He wasn't responsible for her safety.

*Keep telling yourself that, bud.*

Something about the vulnerability he'd witnessed in her had his protective instincts kicking into high gear.

He hurried back downstairs. Caleb was already in his SUV with the engine running so Brett hopped into the passenger's seat.

On the way to the hospital, Caleb's phone rang again. He answered it using the car's Bluetooth feature, so Brett could hear every word spoken.

"Hansen, what's up?"

"Chief, we received a call from the Jessup Inn this morning. The manager saw the broadcast of the amnesiac woman and identified her as someone who rented a room with them yesterday. They went to check the room and she wasn't there."

Brett's gut clenched. "Did they give a name?"

"They did. She checked in using the name Jaycee Richmond. They're emailing a copy of her driver's license and check-in data to you, Chief."

"Thanks, Hansen."

His phone dinged with the email. Brett pulled the phone from the cradle and opened the email. The woman's face popped up on a driver's license, only it wasn't so beaten up. But it showed the same pretty heart-shaped face, blond hair, brown eyes. It was definitely the same woman.

"At least now we have a name," Caleb said.

He agreed. Maybe now they could figure out what she was doing in Jessup. Her license showed an address in Dallas where his offices were, but it could be an old address. He wanted to find out all he could about Jaycee Richmond and why she had one of his business cards on her.

Brett forwarded the email from the hotel to himself so he could share the information with her. Once they arrived at the hospital, he and Caleb separated. Caleb headed toward the security offices while Brett headed to Jaycee's hospital room.

Jaycee. It was weird using her name.

When he saw her, she looked even worse than the night before. Another bruise had formed on her chin and an ugly red-and-blue hue surrounded her neck. He could even see the finger impressions visible on her neck.

Two officers were snapping pictures of her injuries and collecting samples from her fingernails in the hope that forensics could identify the attacker.

He stepped inside and her eyes lit up at seeing him. He smiled and something fluttered in his chest. It felt good to have someone happy to see him for once. It had been a while since he'd even felt wanted.

He allowed the officers to finish their work then approached her once they'd left. "I heard what happened. How are you?"

She touched the mark on her neck and he wasn't surprised when her voice was raw and scratchy. "Not too good."

"Caleb is pulling the security feeds. We'll find this guy. Are you able to describe the attacker this time?"

She shook her head. "He was wearing a mask over his face. I didn't get a good look at him."

"He might be able to hide his face from you, but the security cameras will capture his image. I doubt he walked out with his face covered." He pulled out his cell phone. "I do have some good news however. A local hotel manager recognized your photograph from the news. He remembered you. Apparently, you checked into the Jessup Inn yesterday. He emailed a copy of your driver's license." He held out the image and she took his phone from him and glanced at it.

"Jaycee Richmond?"

"At least now we know what to call you."

She handed the phone back to him. "I don't even recognize my own name."

He was disappointed. He'd hoped seeing her name would spark something that would return her memory. He had to be patient. He couldn't press her too hard, but the waiting was difficult. He wanted answers.

"I want to go to the hotel. Maybe seeing my belongings will help me remember something."

It was a good suggestion. "Any idea when they're releasing you?"

"The doctor said I could go home today. They diagnosed a slight concussion but believe my amnesia is likely the result of the trauma."

It seemed early to let her go, especially given the fresh attack but he wasn't about to argue the point. The sooner she was mobile, the sooner they could find answers to what had happened. And he needed to get someone at the ranch to bring him his car since he'd ridden to the hospital with Caleb. "I'll go see if we can put a rush on the release paperwork, then we'll head to the hotel."

He headed out to the nurses' desk and made the request. "We're working on it now," the head nurse assured him. "It won't be long."

"Does she need to stay with the fresh injuries?" he asked.

"No, she can recuperate from that at home as well as she can here."

He didn't bother reminding her that Jaycee didn't know where her home was. Then he remembered the address on the driver's license. After the hotel, they should check that out. If seeing her stuff at the hotel didn't jog her memory, maybe seeing her own furniture would.

Brett pulled out his cell phone. His nerves were on edge. Why did this woman have his business card and what could have happened to her that would have someone trying to hurt her?

He dialed Wilson Jarrett, his business partner, but he didn't answer. It rolled right over to voice mail. Wilson was known to let his cell phone die. It was a bad habit. So Brett tried the main office line instead, hoping to reach him that way.

The receptionist answered the phone. “B&W Security.”

“Trish, it’s Brett. I’m trying to get hold of Wilson.”

“Then you have great timing because he’s standing here at the reception desk. Hang on.” He heard a beep and knew she’d placed his call on speaker before he heard Wilson’s voice.

“Brett, how’s it going?”

“Not too good, Wilson. I have a dilemma. On my way to my grandfather’s ranch, I came across this woman. She’d been attacked. She had my business card on her. Has anyone been by looking for me lately?”

“Besides the slew of reporters wanting a comment on the Whitney Warren case? Nah. No one’s been here.”

“Actually, a woman did come by,” Trish interrupted. “It was two days ago. She was looking for you, Brett. Said she had something very important to talk to you about. I tried to cover for you and told her you were out of town but she wouldn’t take no for an answer. I called Mitch to escort her out but she left before he had to.”

Mitch Dearborn, one of their security experts on the payroll.

So Jaycee had come looking for him. It was possible she’d somehow gotten ahold of one of his cards while she was at his office and Trish had turned away to call for assistance, but what was so important that she would cause such a scene?

“Why didn’t you tell me?” Wilson asked her over the line.

“I was going to but you’ve also been out of the office for the past two days.”

Wilson's tone lowered. "I was trying to do damage control to our business. You still should have told me."

"She left and, besides, she didn't seem like a reporter to me."

"Did she give a name or leave a number?" Brett asked her.

"No number, but she did say her name was Jaycee… something. I can't remember the last name. I remember Jaycee because it was different."

"What did this woman look like, Trish?" Brett asked.

"Pretty but not dolled-up. About five-seven with blond hair and brown eyes. She dressed like she was doing her best not to draw attention to herself."

He glanced through the window in the door at the woman lying in the hospital bed. It had to have been her who'd come to the office. But how had she tracked him down? "Did you tell her I was headed to Jessup?"

"Absolutely not, Brett. You know me better than that."

He believed her. Trish took her job seriously and vetted everyone who came through the door. She provided as good security for the firm as he and Wilson did for their clients.

Well…used to provide for their clients.

"Thanks, Trish. Thanks, Wilson."

But Wilson wasn't through. "What's going on, Brett? Do I need to come down there?"

"No, not yet. I'm not sure what's happening here, but I'll keep you informed."

He ended the call with his partner then turned back to stare at the woman he'd nearly run down last night.

She'd showed up at his office looking for him and somehow she'd figured out he was going to be in Jessup. Whoever she was, she was good at tracking people because he'd done everything he could to remain under the radar to avoid the press who were constantly contacting him for a quote for their stories about Whitney.

Yet Jaycee Richmond had found him—but not before whatever she'd gotten into or whomever was chasing her had found her.

Jaycee was dressed and ready to go when Brett returned to the room with her discharge papers. She was anxious to go examine the hotel room she'd checked into. Hopefully, it would provide some answers about why she'd been in town and who was after her.

She instinctively touched her neck, remembering the earlier assault. It had been terrifying. She needed to figure out quickly why someone wanted her dead and what her connection was to Brett.

She climbed into Brett's car and tried to settle her mind. "Are you sure you're up for this?" he asked.

She nodded and took a deep breath. "I need to do this."

He drove to the Jessup Inn and they got out. This place didn't spark any memories for her as she stared up at the building. They entered and took the stairs to the third floor, where the manager had indicated her room was. She followed Brett to the room at the end of the hall. Crime scene tape covered the door in an X fashion. It wasn't until she was closer that she noticed the door had been busted, as if someone had burst inside.

She shuddered at the thought. Brett pulled one side of the tape down as he walked inside.

Jaycee took a deep breath as she entered the room. Belongings were scattered on the floor and the dresser had been knocked over. It was obvious she'd been in a fight for her life here, yet she could remember none of it.

Brett watched her closely. "Anything coming back to you?"

She shook her head. "Nothing."

He pointed to the dresser. "I spoke to Caleb earlier when he brought my car to the hospital. He gave me the low down on what they found here. The forensics team discovered blood on the edge of it. They think that might be what you hit your head on during the struggle." He turned to the door. "If you were at the door and your attacker burst inside, you could have been knocked backward into it."

She nodded. That made sense and she could imagine that happening. Yet she didn't know if it had.

"There was also a busted lamp on the floor. Forensics took it for testing. Looks like there might have been some blood on it too along with your fingerprints. You might have used it to fight him off, gotten away and jumped into the car."

And crashed it. Some getaway. She crossed her arms and rubbed them. At least she had gotten away that time and earlier this morning. Would she be so fortunate the next time?

"We didn't find your cell phone or laptop here. Those were found in the debris of the wrecked car. However," he continued, "we did find this." He held up a photo of a handgun. The markers indicated they'd found it in the corner of the room. "Caleb and his team ran it for prints. They found yours all over it. Additionally, the gun appears to be registered to you."

So she'd been so frightened of whatever she was running from that she'd armed herself.

*Great. That doesn't make me feel any better about this situation.*

Or maybe she was just a person who typically carried a handgun. She had no idea. But she'd come to town with it knowing that she was in danger, and that danger had caught up to her. "Whatever was going on, I was obviously scared."

"I'd say you had a reason to be. Someone did burst in here and attack you."

She shuddered, recalling that feeling of the pillow pressing into her, cutting off her air supply. No way to get around that. Someone wanted her dead.

"Caleb said this was a crime scene, but if you want to grab some clothes or belongings, that would be fine. They've already gone through everything. And the hotel has offered you another room on a different floor."

She didn't like the idea that people she didn't know had been through her things, but she didn't exactly have an attachment to them either. She grabbed a few pairs of clothes and some toiletries then stuffed them into a bag. She hadn't brought much with her and that struck her as odd. She must have come here on a whim. But why? And why couldn't she remember?

As Brett led her down the hallway to the elevators,

she noticed the other doors. "Did anyone hear anything when I was attacked?"

"According to Caleb's investigative team, there were only two other guests on this floor. One had her TV up and claims she didn't hear anything. The other guest was out most of the night. No one knew anything was wrong until the manager saw the newscast about you replay this morning and recognized you as a customer he checked in yesterday. He sent someone to check the room. That's when they saw the door kicked in and called the police."

So, if that newscast hadn't played, she might not even know who she was. But then, had that also been the catalyst for the killer to return to finish her off at the hospital? Probably so.

The hotel staff were all kind but she felt their stares. She took the key to a different room then stowed her bag of belongings there and changed out of the scrubs the hospital had offered her before following Brett back to his car. His cousin wanted to see them both at the police station.

When they arrived, Caleb met them with a grim face. "We found a bill of sale inside the crashed vehicle's glove compartment. Looks like you bought it from Russell Stewart the day before yesterday. I contacted him. He claims not to know you personally, but says he posted the car for sale and you answered the ad. Paid cash for it. I also found more information about you, Jaycee. Your prints were on file because you own a cybersecurity business." He spun the laptop on his desk around to show her the website. Her face wasn't displayed, but her name was prominent on the site.

And she noticed it didn't specify what types of cybersecurity jobs she handled.

"According to the reviews, you're good at your job."

She stood up, mulling over this new development. "You're in security, Brett. Were we working on something together?"

"Cybersecurity is a hot business," Brett stated. "I've never heard of you or your company before. As far as I know, we've never used your services, but I can check with my business partner to make sure."

"You should also check out her apartment," Caleb suggested. "If the hotel didn't bring back any memories to you, maybe being in your own place will. I wrote down the address from your driver's license."

Brett took it and nodded. "I had the same idea myself." He turned to Jaycee. "Do you feel up for a ride?"

She nodded. "If it will help me get back my memories and figure out what is going on, I'm up for just about anything."

The four-hour drive to Dallas was long and Brett left the radio on to fill the silence in the air. They didn't have much to say to one another as she watched the landscape pass by.

They reached the address Caleb had given them and the landlord recognized her immediately. "Jaycee, everyone's been worried about you. Someone reported hearing shots from your apartment two nights ago. The police came and found bullet holes and you missing. What happened?"

So she'd been attacked previously at her apartment. Not good. "I'm not sure. All I know is someone is after me. I don't remember what happened." She introduced Brett. "He's trying to help me figure out what's going on."

"Well, I'm glad you're safe." He handed her a spare key and she and Brett walked to the second-floor apartment.

Upon entering, she saw evidence of a struggle here too. Her furniture was overturned and it looked like someone had trashed the place. Brett glanced at a series of holes in the wall. "Bullet holes."

Someone had shot at her here just as her landlord had said.

She moved to where several computer monitors had been shoved off the desk to the floor and smashed. She knelt beside them and picked out several pieces, her brain instinctively putting them together like a puzzle. "A lot of this hardware can be replaced. This is a hard drive. I might be able to recover whatever was on it. It looks like someone tried to smash it, but the data could still be intact."

"Do you remember how to do that?"

"I think so." The chinks in her memory were odd. She remembered computers but couldn't even remember her own name. "I'd like a chance to try anyway. It's possible that whatever was on this is the reason someone is trying to kill me. He must have tried to destroy it by smashing it."

He nodded. "That's a good idea. Figure out what you need and we'll go to the store."

She looked around her apartment. Nothing here

sparked a memory. It was like it was someone else's home. She glanced at the photos on the wall and saw images of herself with a man and a woman.

"Are these my parents, do you think? They might be worried about me. Maybe they can answer some of my questions."

"I doubt that." He handed her what looked like a bookmark, but she saw that it was an obituary for two people who'd died in a house fire. "It was pinned to the refrigerator with a magnet."

She read through it. Robert and Cara Richmond had been killed when their house burned down three years ago. They were survived by their only child, Jaycee. No other family was mentioned in the write-up.

Jaycee felt a wave of sadness at learning about their deaths. She didn't remember them, but they must have been important to her. It looked like she had no family remaining. "I'm alone," she stated.

Brett put his hand on her shoulder. "I'm sorry."

"I don't even remember if I have friends or a boyfriend or anything."

"I don't see pictures of anyone other than your parents. No evidence of a husband or a boyfriend."

So far, this trip down memory lane had her wondering if her life was even worth remembering.

"Let's grab the stuff you need and get out of here," Brett said. "I want to stop by the local police department. They might have information about the previous attack here or if you made any reports of someone harassing you before this happened."

That was a good idea.

Jaycee gathered up the important computer pieces

and placed them into a duffel bag. She also grabbed a few changes of clothing and added them too.

She glanced into the refrigerator and saw evidence of a lot of take-out containers and little food in the cupboards. Apparently, she wasn't a great cook either. Her life pre-amnesia wasn't turning out to be all that memorable.

Brett picked up the duffel bag and they started to walk out, but at the last minute, Jaycee decided to take the memorial bookmark of her parents. She turned back to grab it off the coffee table, bent over, and felt something whiz past her.

"Get down," Brett hollered, shoving her to the floor as another round of gunfire broke the glass in the window and bullets whistled by. She heard them slam into the wall behind her.

Her heart raced and she felt Brett's pounding as well. "Stay down," he commanded her. He crawled to the door and pulled his weapon, firing back at the shooter.

The bullets ceased coming at her as Brett fired several rounds. "I see him across the street. We have to get out of here. Do you have a back door?"

"I don't know!"

She grabbed the duffel where he'd dropped it and the memorial bookmark and army-crawled to him. Once out of the line of fire of the window, she jumped to her feet. Brett grabbed her arm and pulled her toward the back of the apartment through the kitchen as the gunfire continued.

Thankfully, there was a back door. Jaycee pulled it open and hurried down the steps as fast as she could.

Brett pushed at her from behind, urging her to go faster. A faint memory of previously running from her apartment came back to her as they reached the alleyway. This was where it had all started. Someone had attacked her here at her apartment, but she still didn't know why.

Brett ducked behind the front of a pickup truck parked in the alley and pulled her down beside him. He was breathing heavy though his attention was on her. "Are you hurt?"

She shook her head as she did her best to settle her own racing heart. "I'm okay. I wasn't hit." Terror raced through her at the idea that someone had followed them here to shoot at her. "What do we do now?" The shooting had stopped yet she couldn't be certain they were out of danger. The shooter might be waiting for them to show themselves again before he started firing once more.

Or he might have stopped firing because he was coming to find them just to finish them off.

Brett pulled her close to him. She was glad he was there, glad that she had someone she could depend on now. She didn't remember being alone but seeing how isolated her life seemed to be made her glad she wasn't in this by herself any longer.

"Did you see who was shooting at us?"

He shook his head. "I saw the barrel of a rifle. That's all. We have to get out of here, but my Charger is right in the fire zone. The police should be on their way. Surely, someone has called them by now. All we have to do is lay low."

He pulled his gun and morphed into protective mode,

ready if needed. Time seemed to slip by and all she heard were the cries of fear from her neighbors and the pounding of her beating heart.

"I'm sorry I pulled you into this," she said. "I'm sure you're probably wishing you'd left me on the side of that road."

He shook his head. "This is what I do, Jaycee. I protect people. That's probably why you were coming to see me."

"I was coming to see you?" That was news to her. All she knew was that she'd had his business card on her when she'd been attacked.

"I called my office. The receptionist remembers you coming there, looking for me. She said you were very insistent that you needed to get in touch."

So she'd been searching for Brett. She clutched her duffel. Whatever was on that hard drive—or had been once—was probably the reason for all of this.

"I need to find out what is on my drive," she said.

He nodded. "I agree, but first we have to get out of here without getting shot." He grunted. "Where are those cops?"

Moments later, sirens filled the air and Brett relaxed. Jaycee breathed a sigh of relief when the first patrol car arrived at the scene.

Brett holstered his gun and turned to her. "We'll have to give a statement to the police, and I'm sure they'll want to ask questions and look at your apartment. Don't mention the drive you placed in your bag. They might want it as evidence and we need it."

She nodded. That was good thinking. She didn't want

the police to confiscate her hard drive. She needed whatever was on it to give her a clue as to why all this was happening.

Brett continued. “Once we deal with this, we’ll head to my office and you can try to recover your drive. Don’t worry, Jaycee. We’ll figure out why this is happening.”

She waited as he approached an officer to explain what had happened. It felt good to have someone else on her side.

It felt even better to have Brett tell her he would stay with her until they figured out who wanted her dead and why.

# THREE

Brett stepped up to one of the officers who'd arrived and explained what had happened. As he'd expected, one of the neighbors had called in about an active shooter. The patrolman pushed him back to a safe distance while the scene was being secured.

Brett glanced back at Jaycee. She'd taken cover inside the unlocked pickup to keep from looking conspicuous. He was worried about her and what she'd gotten into that had someone targeting her this way. Had this shooter been sitting in wait for her to return to her apartment? Or worse, had they been followed as they'd driven from Jessup to Dallas? He hadn't noticed any cars tailing them and he'd been on guard for that, especially after the attack on her at the hospital.

Once the scene was secure, the officer in charge approached him. "I was told by my patrolman that you have some knowledge of what occurred here?"

Brett showed him his identification, which included his security credentials. "I was accompanying the lady who lives here. She was attacked twice yesterday in Jessup. You can call the local chief of police to confirm that. She's suffering from amnesia from the trauma, so we came back to her apartment to try to figure out what happened to her. Someone started shooting, so we ran out the back and took cover."

"I'll need to speak with her too," the officer stated.

Brett waved her over and she got out and walked toward them. "She wasn't found with any identification on her but her landlord can verify she is who she says. He gave us a spare key about an hour ago."

Brett stepped back as Jaycee approached and let the police officer take her statement about what occurred. He tried to press her for answers about what happened in her apartment previously but she insisted she didn't remember. Brett had been hoping something like this might have jogged her memory.

Oh well.

He was glad to see she'd left the duffel bag at the truck. He'd meant what he'd said about the police wanting to take her computer drive as evidence. They could have the rubble that remained upstairs. If he and Jaycee had any chance of figuring all this out, it hinged on her getting data from that drive. If she couldn't remember, he really needed that information to tell them something.

The officer called him forward. "Detective Hennessy is enroute to the scene. He'll want to speak to you both again once he arrives."

Brett tensed at the name. Hennessy was the lead detective on Whitney's case. Of course, it had to be him. He'd be thrilled to learn Brett was involved in yet another shooting. He rubbed his face and braced himself. Hennessy had drilled him good in his questioning about the circumstances of Whitney's murder. The man had blamed him and Brett couldn't even say he was wrong.

He glanced at Jaycee and all the fear and uncertainty he'd been reliving flooded him. He'd gone back through his security procedures step-by-step in the past few weeks. He'd missed something and that had cost Whitney her life.

What was he thinking believing he could keep another woman safe?

He would do better to drop her off at the office and let Wilson handle Jaycee's case. Only he couldn't get past the fact that she'd been trying to find *him*. She'd stood in his office where eight security specialists had been available for hire and demanded to see him.

He braced himself a half hour later when he heard Hennessy's voice and saw him approaching. "Well, well, well. Why am I not surprised to see you here, Harmon? Trouble seems to follow you around, doesn't it?"

He couldn't prove it but Brett was certain Hennessy was leaking information about him to the press. It was the only way some of those reports about Whitney's failed security could have come to light.

"Detective Hennessy. I'm surprised you're involved in this case. This is Jaycee Richmond. She was the one being shot at."

He gave her a nod of greeting. "You might want to rethink your security if you're relying on this fellow, ma'am."

Brett clenched his fists at his sides and bit his tongue

at that remark. His face warmed and he was certain he was turning red with embarrassment. Now wasn't the time for Hennessy to malign his abilities.

He glanced over at Jaycee, expecting a look of doubt on her face. A man with a badge had just insinuated he wasn't good at his job. Would she question his ability to keep her safe now?

Instead of moving away, she took a step closer to him. "Actually, I feel very safe with him, Detective."

A wave of gratitude rushed through Brett and bolstered his confidence. "Did you find the person shooting at us, Detective?"

He sighed and folded his arms. "Not yet. Witnesses claim they saw a man shooting from an apartment across the street from Miss Richmond's. No one got a good look at him and we've verified with the tenant that the apartment was supposed to be empty all day. We're gathering some spent bullet casings and have fingerprinted the apartment, but it sure would help if we knew why this guy is targeting you, Miss Richmond."

Jaycee got that deer-in-the-headlights look at Hennessy's question. "I—I don't know. I don't remember why all this is happening to me."

"One of my officers noted that you were attacked in your apartment two days ago and that now you have amnesia?" His tone had a hint of incredulity and Brett felt the need to defend her.

"She was nearly killed twice in Jessup. I brought her back here, hoping she would remember who's after her, but, so far, nothing has returned to her," Brett told him.

"Did she make any reports of anyone harassing her or breaking into her apartment prior to two days ago?"

Hennessy shook his head. "No. I had someone double-check that. We don't have any calls or reports taken on or about Jaycee Richmond before the attack in her apartment. If someone was bothering her, she didn't alert the police."

Brett sighed, disappointed that there wasn't a paper trail for them to follow up on. Whatever had happened to shove her into danger's path must have come on suddenly.

"You know how to reach me if you uncover anything," Brett said.

Hennessy nodded but gave one final shot. "Try to do a better job keeping this one alive."

Brett bit back a reply. It wouldn't do any good for Jaycee's case for him to engage with Hennessy. He just wanted the detective to do his job and arrest Whitney's killer and find Jaycee's attacker.

"Let's go," he said, urging Jaycee back toward the truck where they'd taken cover. "Let's head to my offices so you can get to work on your hard drive."

"I'll need some new equipment," she reminded him.

He nodded. "We'll pick up whatever you need." He stopped, grabbed the duffel then hustled her toward his Charger, doing his best to keep the bag out of view in case Hennessy wanted to see what was in it. The sooner they were away from this scene and Hennessy, the better.

He didn't want Jaycee getting the wrong idea about him.

"That detective doesn't like you very much, does

he?" Jaycee asked once they were in the car and on the road.

Brett gripped the steering wheel. "No, he doesn't."

"How come?"

He didn't want to tell her and risk her doubting him, but he knew she would eventually learn about Whitney. "I had a client who was killed. Hennessy blames me. He thinks it was my fault."

"Was it?"

He grimaced then shrugged and told her the truth he'd been grappling with. "I'm not sure. I thought I did everything right, but the killer managed to circumvent my security systems. I haven't figured out how yet."

She reached across the seat and touched his arm. "I'm sure you did everything you could."

Her understanding was almost too much for him. In the past three weeks, he'd endured threats and smears of his reputation. No one had been on his side except for Wilson and the others in his company. They'd stood by him despite the fact that his actions had affected their reputations, too, by default. Business hadn't just slowed down, it had skidded to a stop.

No one wanted to place their security in the hands of someone who'd allowed a murderer to get to his client.

No one but Jaycee.

But she wasn't even in her right mind. If it wasn't for the amnesia, she, too, would probably be looking elsewhere for help.

He'd been doing a lot of questioning of God in the past few weeks since Whitney died. Wondering why He'd allowed it to happen and if He'd been punishing

Brett for something. But now Brett needed Him and, instead of demanding answers, he was asking for help.

*Please help me keep Jaycee safe. Please, God, don't let me fail her the way I failed Whitney.*

They stopped by an electronics store where Brett purchased a laptop and other equipment Jaycee needed to reconstruct her system. She promised to repay him for the purchases once she remembered which bank she used, but he waved away her concerns. He wanted answers too.

She couldn't get the confrontation between Brett and that Detective Hennessy from her mind. She hadn't liked the detective much, and it had less to do with the way he'd pressured her to try to remember than his attitude toward Brett. After all, he hadn't been the one to pull the trigger that killed that woman and Jaycee was sure Brett had done everything he could to keep her safe.

She had to believe that now that she was also depending on him to keep her alive.

She spotted several news vans parked outside the B&W Security building as they approached. Reporters obviously camping out, hoping for a comment to add to their news story. Brett ignored them and sped right past, turning into a parking garage exclusively for the tenants of the building where his office was housed. Yet, she'd seen him notice the vans and tense as they drove by.

They parked and hurried toward an elevator that took them upstairs to the B&W Security offices. "Welcome to B&W Security." He seemed proud of the name on the door and opened it for her. She stepped into an office with plush carpeting and a reception desk front and center. A woman with glasses and long brown hair stood when they entered and Jaycee had a sudden flashback to being here before and meeting her.

"That's her," the woman proclaimed. "The woman who was looking for you." She walked around the desk and spoke to Jaycee. "It's nice to see you again. I see you found Brett."

She tried to laugh off the nervousness. "I did. Thank you."

"This is Trish, our receptionist. Trish, this is Jaycee Richmond. We're working on something together. I'm going to set her up in the conference room."

She nodded. "Wilson asked to see you when you arrived. I can show Jaycee the way."

He hesitated, obviously not wanting to leave her side. Jaycee assured Brett she would be fine. What harm could come to her in a conference room? Besides, she didn't want to monopolize his time. He still had a business to run.

He transferred the duffel bag, new laptop and bag full of computer parts they'd picked up on the way here to her. "I'll check on you in a few minutes to see if you need anything."

"I'll be fine."

She walked behind Trish, who led her down a long hallway before pushing open a door. The room had a long table that took up most of the space but it also held a side bar with glasses and water, a few plants, and a large-screen TV on the wall. "Make yourself comfortable," the woman told her. "No one's going to bother you in here. The kitchen is right next door. Feel free to help yourself. If you need anything, just press zero on the phone. It'll connect you right to my desk."

"Thank you for your help."

"No problem," Trish stated before walking out and closing the door behind her.

Jaycee sighed and glanced around the room. She did feel safer now that they were at the security office. No one would bother her in here.

She unpacked the new laptop and the tools she'd purchased to try to reassemble the hard drive she'd found at her apartment, and had no trouble locating an outlet or computer port. It still struck her as odd that she seemed to know what she was doing when it came to computers, yet she couldn't even remember her cell phone number or her favorite color. The doctor had assured her it might all come back to her, but she was impatient. She didn't like the feeling of not knowing anything at all about her life. She felt helpless and out of control, two emotions she didn't have to recover her memories to know she didn't like.

She pulled out some cords and hooked up the hard drive to her new laptop then started digging into the system.

Most of the files were damaged but she was able to pull up a few and search through them. They were mostly random files she didn't understand out of context. One was a program to test and determine random-number sequences while another bypassed security alerts in automated systems.

Those seemed like odd things to have on her computer but Jaycee supposed it had something to do with her work. Cybersecurity encompassed a lot of different aspects, from network monitoring to encryption software to analyzing and preventing security breaches.

She needed more information about what exactly she did.

A quick view of her website provided minimal detail. Most of the information contained there was ambiguous and vague computer speak, which made her believe she either did whatever work came her way, or she specialized in something she preferred not to advertise. Either way, it seemed odd for a computer specialist to have a website that provided such little information.

A contact email listed on her website gave her another option for digging into her life however. She took the email address and managed to search for it on the hard drive.

Bingo!

Excitement rushed through her as several email conversations began popping up on her screen. Now, she was getting somewhere.

She read through a number of emails she'd exchanged with a man named Joe Cleveland in which they talked about overriding a security alarm system.

She swallowed hard. Some of the data was missing but she was able to piece together enough of the bits to know she did not like the context of the conversations. They essentially detailed how she had overridden safety protocols to place the security system into sleep mode. Another email with someone named Harry Jackson discussed security protocols at a bank called First United.

Jaycee pulled her hands away from the keyboard.

She recognized hacking techniques when she saw them. And she'd performed those acts. She'd hacked into a bank as well as someone's security system.

She was a criminal.

No wonder her website provided so little detail. It was probably a front for her criminal enterprises to make herself look respectable.

She covered her face with her hands as her mind spun with this new information. She didn't feel like a thief. But she had definitely bypassed someone's security protocols and who but a thief would do such a thing?

Had she trashed her own apartment to cover her tracks? The man who'd attacked her had definitely been real. Was he one of her victims trying to exact revenge?

A knock sounded on the door, causing her heart to jump into her throat. She quickly minimized the screen just as Brett poked his head in.

"Find anything?" he asked.

Jaycee gulped at his question, which sounded oddly like an accusation now that she knew what she was. No way was she going to admit to being a criminal, at least not until she knew more about her system and her life. "Nothing yet, but I'm still working."

"Okay. Keep me posted. My office is just down the hall. It's after six so most everyone is leaving for the day. It'll just be us here. I thought I'd order in some supper for us."

"Sounds good," she told him even though the thought of food made her stomach roil. She blew out a breath when he closed the door behind him. That had been close. Brett trusted her. He still believed in her. What would he do when he discovered what she truly was? She didn't even want to think about that.

She stared at the computer screen before bringing the drive window back up. She needed more information. Had this been a once-or-twice kind of thing? Or was she a career criminal? She already knew of at least two hacking incidents.

She swallowed hard, uncertain she wanted to know the answer.

She turned back to the computer and continued her search, relieved when she spotted a file containing invoices for her services. The name on one invoice was Joe Cleveland, the same name she'd traded emails with about hacking into a security system. Was this man her partner? No, he wouldn't have paid her if he was. And what kind of criminal sent invoices for their services?

From what she could piece together from this data, she'd been hired by Joe Cleveland to hack into his business and bypass security measures. Maybe she wasn't a thief, then, but certainly a hacker for hire for unscrupulous business owners. That wasn't much better.

She needed to find out more about this man and why he'd needed her hacking skills.

She pulled up file after file on the damaged drive but found each one more corrupt than the next. She managed to pull together bits and bytes of email conversations and data files, but little else.

Then she spotted a name that sank her.

B&W Security.

That was this company. Brett's security firm.

The pieces suddenly clicked into place.

She'd hacked into Brett's security system.

And she'd gone to a lot of trouble to specifically track Brett down. Was this the reason?

Panic suddenly gripped her. Brett was being blamed for letting a killer murder Whitney Warren.

Her fingers flew across the keyboard as she searched for dates of when this job she'd been hired to do had taken place.

Could it be?

No, no, no…

*Please don't let the dates match!*

She checked the date on the invoice then pulled up a celebrity news website and skimmed through a story about Whitney Warren's murder.

Tears filled her eyes when she realized the dates were a perfect match.

She pushed to her feet and pressed her hand against her mouth to keep from crying out at the realization of what she'd done.

She'd infiltrated Brett's security system the same date Whitney was killed.

She'd been the one to bring down his security systems.

Brett wasn't responsible for Whitney's death.

She was.

# FOUR

Jaycee's hands shook as she approached the door to Brett's office the next morning. He'd arranged for her to spend the night in a hotel but sleep hadn't come easily as her mind had continued to run through the information she'd uncovered. She'd double checked her findings again this morning only to discover she hadn't been wrong. Everything she'd recovered pointed to her hacking into a B&W security system on the night Whitney had been murdered.

She'd printed off the pieces of recovered data that showed her hacking into a bank system and transferring money, and the one showing her involvement in breaching B&W's security measures and putting the system on sleep mode while Whitney was being killed.

She couldn't hold on to this information. She had to come clean to Brett. He deserved to know the truth about the night Whitney died. She just wished she didn't have to be the one to tell him. He was the only person she remembered who'd been on her side. Who'd stood up for her.

Once he knew the truth of her involvement, she wasn't so sure that would continue.

*Open the door, Jaycee. The truth will set you free.*

Where had she heard that nonsense before? In this case, the truth would send her right out the door.

She spun around and headed for the conference room. She couldn't do it. But she knew in her soul that she had to.

She turned back to his office and nearly knocked him down when Brett opened the door and stepped out.

"Jaycee, did you find something?"

The anticipation in his face defeated her. "I did find something." Her hand shook as she handed him the invoice she'd uncovered from Joe Cleveland. "It's a payment for a job I did."

His face clouded as he read the paper. "This says you were hired to hack into one of the security systems of B&W. Our security systems that we provide for our clients' safety?"

She nodded. "And look at the date, Brett."

His jaw clenched. "The night Whitney died."

She took a deep breath as his eyes bore into hers.

"You hacked into one of our security systems the night Whitney was killed."

Tears pressed against her eyes but she forced them back. Now wasn't the time to fall apart in front of him. It might elicit some kind of sympathy and she didn't deserve that. "It's my fault that Whitney died. I was the one who bypassed your system."

He walked into his office. He tossed the sheet of paper onto his desk then ran a hand through his hair. "I can't believe this is happening." He picked up the paper again. "Someone paid you to do this? Why would you take that job?" He stared at her like he was legitimately expecting an answer.

"I don't know. I can't remember."

His tone turned hard and scornful. "Well, that's very convenient."

She bristled at the implied accusation. "It's not a lie, Brett. You know I've lost my memory. Do you think I would have gone through all of this if I hadn't? You had no reason to doubt me earlier."

"That's because I didn't know that you'd hacked into my system and gotten a friend of mine killed." He blew out a breath and turned away from her.

She sank into a chair. Tears welling, she choked them back. He was right. She was responsible for the death of that woman.

She folded her hands together and put forth an effort to keep her composure. "I don't expect any sympathy from you. I can't believe what I did. I wish I could remember why I did it, but I don't." She stood to face him. "You don't have to worry about me any longer. I'll gather my things and get out of your hair for good."

She headed for the door, already wondering where she would go. Back to her apartment, she guessed, although she didn't know how safe it would be there. That didn't matter. She was on her own now.

"Wait," Brett said as she reached the door.

She turned back to face him. He was holding the paper she'd given him. "This is an invoice, which means someone paid you to do this. Who?"

"From what I was able to find, the client's name was Joe Cleveland. I tried looking him up, but it seems like the address and phone number he gave me were fake."

"You don't check these things before you hack into someone's system and endanger other people's lives?"

She did her best to keep her cool. "I do. I know I do." She had no proof of that, but it was a gut feeling. "I dug through my records. He mentioned that someone I know recommended me to him."

He pulled out his chair and took a seat then turned on his computer. "We'll find him and ask him why he wanted you to do this. What was his name again?"

She walked around the desk to look over his shoulder as he opened up the database his company used to gather information. "Joe Cleveland."

He typed in the name but nothing came up.

Jaycee looked through her notes again. "So many of my files are missing but this was the address and phone number he gave me." She called them out and Brett searched through the database once more.

Again, he came up empty. "What about the client that referred him?"

"His name was Harry Jackson." She didn't tell him that she'd also discovered that name in connection with the bank system she'd hacked into. That information could wait until later.

Brett keyed in the name Harry Jackson and his image popped up on the computer screen along with his driver's license photo and employment and credit details. "Says here he's worked at First United Bank for twelve years."

Her heart dropped. Now, he had to know. Where did

the madness end? "I also found some data that suggests I hacked into the system at First United."

Anger brimmed in his eyes as he looked at her then turned back to the computer to focus on Harry Jackson. "No outstanding warrants or legal troubles, but his credit score has recently taken a nosedive." He pressed a few more keys and more information popped up. "Looks like Harry's been hemorrhaging money over the past year. All his credits cards are maxed out and, until a few weeks ago, he was four months behind on his mortgage. He recently made large payments to cover his debts."

As she stared at the photo on the screen, a vague memory of Harry popped up. He'd always seemed to be a decent guy. "I wonder what we were up to?" Had they robbed that bank together? Or had she duped him?

Brett stood and clicked off his computer. "We'll go ask him first thing tomorrow. Someone may have paid him big to recommend Joe Cleveland to you. Or else he's in on it, too, and can provide me some answers."

So he wasn't kicking her out. He still needed her…at least for now. The relief of that nearly did her in. "Can you give me a minute to freshen up?"

He nodded and pointed to a door on the inner wall. "Use my private bathroom. I'll be waiting for you up front at the reception desk."

She washed her face and did her best to make sure her eyes weren't red. She felt better having gotten the truth out there but she still didn't know why she'd taken such risks. Was it really all about the money? She stared at herself in the mirror. Was she so greedy that she would endanger a woman's life for a payday?

Oh how she wished she could remember!

She would uncover the truth one way or another, although she wasn't so certain she would like what she discovered about herself once it was all said and done.

Brett struggled to keep his cool as he waited for Jaycee. He hated how he'd reacted to her revelation. That wasn't the type of person he wanted to be. Discovering she was a hacker wasn't the way he'd imagined this scenario playing out, but if she couldn't remember doing it, did it really make her a bad person?

What he couldn't get past was the fact that someone had paid her to do this, paid her to dig into his systems and undermine Whitney's protections. He needed to know who that person was. People in Whitney's business would have had the money to pull off this elaborate plan. He wondered briefly if he should contact Detective Hennessy with this new information.

Ultimately, he decided he would wait to contact the detective after they went to question this Harry Jackson. Perhaps their evidence, including Jaycee's involvement, could finally bring Whitney the justice she deserved.

Her eyes were red when she emerged from the bathroom. He felt like a heel. He needed to direct his anger toward someone else. He didn't know Jaycee that well, but what he knew of her so far, she didn't seem like the type of person who would be part of a conspiracy to murder someone. Yet she had, and then she'd tried to find him afterward.

Why?

Maybe this bank manager could shed some light on that question.

They climbed into his Charger and drove to the downtown headquarters of First United Bank. He ushered Jaycee inside then asked to see Harry Jackson. The receptionist picked up the phone and made a call. A moment later, Brett saw a man walk out of an office, spot them then hurry back inside and shut the door.

He took Jaycee's elbow. "There."

The receptionist called to them to wait but Brett's attention had been piqued. The name on the door was Harry Jackson. Brett pushed open the door and stepped inside as Jaycee followed.

Harry Jackson stood in the corner of his office, sweating in his expensive suit. He turned to look at Jaycee and his face paled. "No, you can't be here again. You both need to leave right now."

"I don't think so," Brett said. He closed the door to give them privacy. They were definitely in the right place.

"I've already told you everything I know, Jaycee."

"You have? When?"

"Don't play games with me. You came here three days ago and read me the riot act. I told you then everything I knew about Joe Cleveland. I don't know anything else to tell you."

She stepped up. "Well, you're going to have to, Harry. Something happened to me. Someone attacked me and tried to kill me. As a result, I have big chunks of my memory missing, including our conversation."

Harry's eyes widened and, if possible, his face lost

even more color. "What? He tried to kill you?" Panic filled his face. "You didn't say anything about that when you were here before."

So she must have confronted Jackson before the apartment shooting.

"I really can't be involved in this."

"Well, you are involved," Brett interrupted. "Why don't you tell us both everything you told Jaycee three days ago. Don't leave anything out."

"How do you know me?" Jaycee demanded. "And who is this Joe Cleveland?"

He nervously straightened his tie and mopped sweat from his forehead. "I don't know his real name. That's the name he gave me. We met in Gamblers Anonymous."

"You've got a gambling problem?"

He nodded. "I was down a lot of money. In way over my head. I met this guy and we got into a conversation. I don't remember how or why we got on the topic of security, but I mentioned that I knew someone. He wanted your name and wanted me to convince you he was trustworthy. I didn't want to do it."

"But then he offered you money," Brett said, finishing his story for him. He'd heard tales like that one before.

"I was tempted, but by then I suspected he wasn't on the up and up. So he turned to another tactic. Blackmail. He said if I didn't do it, he would tell my bosses and the police that I've been skimming money from accounts to cover my gambling debts."

Jaycee looked at him wide-eyed. "Is that true? Had you been doing that?"

He hung his head in an obvious positive response.

"Did I help you do that? Are we partners?" Worry lined her face as she asked the question.

Brett hadn't even thought of that. How had Jaycee and this Harry Jackson met up?

Jackson insisted otherwise. "No. You had nothing to do with that."

"I found something in my computer." She pulled a sheet of paper from her pocket and showed it to him. Proof that she'd hacked into the bank's systems.

He glanced through it and nodded. "Sure, I've seen this before."

"Then you know what I did."

"Of course. You breached our online security and transferred a hundred thousand dollars from our accounts." He stated it like a fact and didn't even seem fazed by her actions. "I don't understand. This transaction occurred over a year ago and is the reason we upgraded to the new protocols you provided. You were well paid for your services. Are you trying to say you weren't compensated enough? Because my boss is not going to go for that."

Brett leaned forward. "Wait, what do you mean she was well compensated? You wanted her to hack into your systems?"

"We paid her to do so…well, to try to do so. Obviously, she succeeded." He still looked confused by their responses. He reached into his desk drawer, pulled out a business card, and handed it to Brett. "We hired her to test our security protocols. She came highly recommended and did a great job."

Brett read the card then showed it to her. It had her name and, beneath it, the words "security consultant."

"You mean you hired me to do this? I'm not a criminal?" Her voice held a note of hopefulness.

"You were paid to try to transfer money into a dummy account that we set up per your instructions. We had access to it at all times." Understanding dawned on him. "You didn't know this was your job?"

She pressed her hand over her mouth. She looked at Brett and happy tears shone in her eyes. "I'm not a criminal."

He smiled and felt a tinge of relief himself. He hadn't liked seeing her in that light.

But that didn't change the facts of the case.

He turned back to Jackson. "So this Joe Cleveland knew about what Jaycee did for a living?"

Jackson sighed and nodded. "He knew the bank had hired someone. Unfortunately, I couldn't risk his turning me in, so I gave him Jaycee's name and passed him off as a businessman who wanted you to do the same with his company's systems."

Brett felt his ire rise. *His company.* So Jaycee had been tricked into believing she was performing a test of the security systems.

"Needless to say, I took the money and did as he asked. I'm sorry, Jaycee, if it got you into some kind of trouble. I didn't mean to hurt you. I was just desperate."

"Some kind of trouble?" Brett had to laugh to keep from losing his cool. "Because of what you did, someone died. Whoever your mysterious Joe Cleveland was, he murdered or caused the murder of a vibrant, kind woman."

Harry Jackson stared at Brett. He gulped hard. Then recognition shone. "You're the guy who was supposed to protect that movie star who was murdered."

"That's right. I am that guy. And because of you, Jaycee was tricked into breaching a firewall to a security system that allowed a murderer to walk in and get to her."

"I-I'm sorry."

Jaycee stood and got between Brett and Harry. "Did you have an address or phone number for this man?"

"I did but the last time I tried to call the number, it was no longer in service. I never had an address."

"Did you meet with him here at the bank? Do you have any videos of this man?"

He thought for a moment then nodded. "Yes, he always came here to the bank. I'll go to the security office and see about getting you a copy." He rushed from the office.

Jaycee turned to Brett and placed her hand against his chest, trying to calm him down. "It'll be okay. We'll find out who this guy is and bring him to justice."

He was surprised by the way his heart kicked up a notch at her touch and he couldn't stop the urge to cover her hand with his. He had to get his head together. He'd nearly spooked this guy Jackson. Without him to steer them toward the man who'd hired Jaycee, they might never discover who'd killed Whitney and pulled them all into this mess.

The shimmer of red still present in her eyes reminded him of how he'd lashed out at her. That hadn't been fair.

She'd been tricked into hacking into his security system. She'd questioned him in his office about whether or not he believed her amnesia was real. He did believe it. And he couldn't wrap his mind around her being anything other than another victim of this killer's sick game.

*Is that the same clear headedness you used with Whitney?*

Brett shook that thought away but it had landed hard. He had been blinded by Whitney, not because of anything romantic going on between them but because of the stardom and fame being around her provided him.

Jackson returned. "The head of security was able to pull video feeds. He loaded the images onto this flash drive." He opened his computer and inserted the drive. They huddled around the computer while the image loaded.

The video showed Jackson speaking with another man. Brett quickly cataloged his details. Six-one. Dark hair. Athletic build. Casual clothing and wearing boots. A baseball cap cast a shadow on his face. He seemed familiar but Brett couldn't get a good enough look to say for sure if he knew him or not.

He glanced at Jaycee, who frowned then shook her head. "I don't recognize him." It might be the memory loss that caused her to not recognize the man, but it was also possible she just had never met him.

Brett ran a hand over the back of his neck as frustration built in him again. "This could be anyone." He glared at Jackson. "Wasn't there a better image? One that showed his face more prominently?"

Jackson shook his head. "No, this was the best one.

He always wore that hat. I think he was trying to avoid the cameras."

It made sense. These days, video surveillance was everywhere. Anyone planning something nefarious would take precautions to avoid cameras even if they didn't plan on getting caught.

"And you're sure he didn't give you any other names besides Joe Cleveland?"

"That's what he called himself. I wasn't exactly in a position to ask for identification, was I?"

He didn't care for Jackson's defensive tone. He'd given a madman Jaycee's name, all to cover himself and his illegal actions. Brett motioned for Jaycee as he pulled a business card from his pocket. "Have your security guy email me a still image of this. And if Cleveland contacts you again, call me. I mean it. I'd better not find out you've been in contact with our prime suspect."

Jackson took the card, sweat beading on his forehead once again. He fidgeted. "About the money I took—"

"We're not cops," Brett told him, "but I would make real sure that money was returned sooner than later."

He heaved a sigh of relief then nodded. "I will. I mean, it will be. Right away."

Brett pulled the flash drive from the computer and pocketed it. They walked off and left Jackson to stew in his own guilt.

Jaycee was indignant as they left the bank. "You're really going to let that guy get away with embezzling from the bank? Especially after what he did to me? He needs to pay for his actions."

He smiled, liking that she'd asked the question. It told

him a lot about her moral center. If her first response to injustice was outrage without her memories, it was a good indication that she was a good person with them. "Well, I don't like to see people get jammed up. I've seen what addiction can do. If he puts the money back, I think this near discovery might set him on the straight and narrow path. If not, I was thinking an anonymous tip to his supervisor might do the trick."

She smiled. "And how will you know if he puts it back?"

"I'll know."

They walked to his car and he opened the passenger's door for her. She slipped inside then he walked around and got in. He slid the flash drive into the console for safekeeping. "I hope this is enough to find our mysterious Mr. Cleveland."

"I can probably find a computer program that will scan the web for his image."

"You can do that?"

She shrugged. "It's actually fairly simple. Google Images might even do the trick. It's worth a shot."

"We have resources at the agency, too, and, barring that, I have cousins in law enforcement. Caleb is the chief of police in Jessup."

"I remember," she reminded him.

"That's right. You might not know my other cousin, Luke, is retired FBI. He might have some contacts that could help us identify the man on this disc. What I don't understand is why this elaborate scheme just to get to Whitney?"

She thought about it then shrugged. "My guess is that

you had her locked down so tightly that he couldn't get to her by any other means."

Had he been so thorough with her security? It hadn't seemed like it in the past few weeks despite the fact that he hadn't been able to discover how the killer had gotten past his safeguards. Now he knew, yet he was still questioning himself. Had he taken every precaution with her safety?

"I gave the police a list with everyone Whitney thought might have a grudge against her. She knew she had a stalker but, at that time, didn't know who it was. My team at B&W had investigated this list when Whitney hired us but nothing came from our initial evaluation of the names. We must have missed something. I still have it on my laptop. We should go back through it. We should also talk with Detective Hennessy again. From what I understand, the man they arrested admitted to stalking Whitney. I want to know more about this guy and if he could be our mysterious Mr. Cleveland." His stomach growled with hunger and he realized he'd been so focused on confronting Jackson that they hadn't even stopped for breakfast. Now, it was lunchtime. "But first, let's get something to eat."

"That sounds good. I'm famished. I felt ill thinking I was some kind of criminal."

He drove to a café and they walked inside and found a table. She ordered soup and salad while he ordered a sandwich and chips. She munched her salad while Brett watched her. He considered himself a fair judge of character and he had a good feeling about Jaycee. Everything he'd learned about her so far told him she was a victim in all of this. Why else would she have been coming to find him except to warn him of what had happened?

It was time he let her off the hook.

He leaned across the table. "I was thinking about this situation and about finding you in Jessup."

She picked up one of his chips and munched on it, but he spotted her nervousness in the way her eye twitched. "What about it?"

"I believe you must have been coming to find me to tell me about what you'd done."

She nodded. "I wondered that myself. Surely, I must have known who was behind this. Naturally, I would want to tell you. But why did I wait so long and why wouldn't I just go to the police with what I knew?"

He shook his head and leaned back in his seat. "Honestly, I don't know why you waited so long. The smart thing to do, especially after someone attacked you in your apartment, would have been to go to the police."

She fiddled with the napkin in her hands. "I can sort of understand why I wouldn't. If I realized what had happened and knew how it had affected you, I might want to explain myself to you before everything came out." She sniffed and rubbed her face. "Maybe to apologize for my role in all of this."

He studied her. She was probably right about her actions, although he suspected she was only guessing at her reasons. The real reason hadn't come back to her yet. "Even at the risk of your own life?"

She shrugged. "I don't know. Maybe." She picked up a pickle and bit into it. "It sounds crazy, I know. Actually, I don't know. I don't know anything." She leaned onto her elbows, put her hands over her temples and groaned in frustration. "Why can't I remember?"

"You've been through a horrific event. It's understandable that you might have some lingering trauma. I'm sure it'll come back to you. And, just to be clear, I don't believe you're faking the amnesia. I'm sorry I ever implied it." He reached across the table and covered her hand with his, doing his best to ignore the softness of her skin.

She gave a weary sigh but closed her hand around his. "I just feel so frustrated. The truth is right there. I feel like I can almost grab it but it's just out of my reach."

"Don't let it stop you, Jaycee. We're going to figure this out. Now that I know someone sabotaged me and Whitney, I won't quit until I uncover who it was. I can't change what happened to her, but I can find her killer and bring him to justice. And I will keep you safe."

She pulled her hand from his to wipe away an errant tear that slid down her cheek. "I was pretty worried you were going to show me the door when you found out what I did."

His face warmed. "I can't say I didn't think about it, but I needed you. I still need you to figure this out. Until we do, you're stuck with me."

Her lips curved upward into a small smile. "That doesn't sound so terrible."

They finished up their meal then walked back to his Charger.

Brett watched her. She was knee-deep in this conspiracy and he honestly believed she hadn't intentionally set out to hurt him or to get Whitney killed.

But that nagging worry wouldn't let go. He didn't know Jaycee and he'd already been burned once. Because of her memory loss, all they could do was speculate on why she'd been coming to find him. He needed to do his due diligence.

He spotted a gas station and pulled into it. "I need to fill up. I'll only be a minute."

He inserted his card into the machine then pumped the gas. But as he was waiting for it to fill, he pulled out his cell and took several large steps away from the car, close enough that he could still see his gas pumping and stop anyone who tried to take advantage, yet far enough away that Jaycee couldn't hear his conversation.

He dialed his cousin. "Caleb, I need to ask you to do me a favor." He could check her credit report back at his own office but he didn't want to put this off. Plus, he didn't want Jaycee to accidentally discover he still didn't trust her because he wanted to trust her more than anything. "Can you run Jaycee's financials? I want to know if she's come into any large sums of money recently."

"Why? What's going on?"

"We've uncovered information that one of Jaycee's jobs is that people hire her to test their security systems. Someone apparently paid her to hack into one of B&W's systems and bring it down the night Whitney died."

"That's terrible. Do you know who hired her?"

"Not yet and her memory is still fuzzy on that. She knows she did it but not why. I'm just doing everything in my power to believe she didn't know that what she was doing was going to put someone's life in danger."

"You think she might have been complicit?"

"I don't think she was but I also can't risk not vetting that possibility. Will you help me?"

Caleb sighed on the other end. "I'll see what I can do. I have some updates for you on the attack at the hospital though. We weren't able to get a good image of Jaycee's attacker and none of the forensics has come back with anything identifiable."

That was disheartening. Brett had been hoping that DNA from the attack could help solve this.

"I'll get back to you on those records when I know something."

"Thanks, cuz." He ended the call, removed the gas nozzle and closed up his tank, then climbed back into the car with Jaycee. He didn't feel good about asking his cousin to check her out, but it was the smart move. After all, he didn't really know her or why she had been coming to see him in Jessup—and at his office. For all they knew, she might have been on her way to kill him. They had found a weapon in her hotel room. But why would she go to such lengths?

Now he really was letting his imagination run wild.

He didn't believe she was a willing participant in this conspiracy but he owed it to himself to do his due diligence. He'd already allowed one person—the killer—past his guard and that had resulted in Whitney's death. He couldn't risk another misstep.

"Everything okay?" Jaycee asked him, her smile warm and innocent.

He nodded in the affirmative. "Yep, everything's good."

He briefed her on his call with Caleb, leaving out the part about asking his cousin to dig deeper into her financials.

*Please, God, don't let this check come back with any issues about Jaycee.*

At the police station, Brett asked for Detective Hennessy and the officer on duty told them to wait in the seating area.

Brett tapped his leg nervously. "I hope he'll see us."

Jaycee hoped so too. She wanted to know more information about Whitney's murder. She still wasn't certain about the plan, though, and pulled Brett aside. "Are we telling this detective about my involvement?"

He thought for a moment. "I think we have to, Jaycee. He needs all the information if he's going to find Whitney's killer."

She wished she remembered more about what really had happened and how she'd gotten involved, but her memory was still so full of holes.

The detective she'd seen at her apartment appeared behind the front desk. He gave a frown then motioned for them to meet him around at a door. He opened it and leaned against it, giving a heavy, irritated sigh. "Not again. What do you want, Harmon?"

"We have information that might help find Whitney's killer."

"That's already taken care of. We arrested a man a few hours ago. He just admitted to stalking and murdering Whitney because he became obsessed with her and she rejected him."

"Who? What's his name?"

Hennessy motioned them through the door and led them to the outside of a holding room where they could see a man sat handcuffed to a table. He had a slight build and wild eyes, in Jaycee's opinion. He looked like a madman.

"What's his name?" Brett asked.

"Lincoln Albertson. He's a maintenance care worker for the town of Chesterfield, Florida."

"Did you find the gun? Or his prints in the hotel room?"

Again, the detective looked irritated. "No, we didn't find the gun. He probably threw it in the river. And he either wiped any prints or wore gloves."

"What proof do you have that he's your guy?" Brett asked.

"Is a confession good enough for you? We also have video of the suspect outside the hotel the night the victim was killed."

Jaycee took a good look at the man again, hoping to spark some sort of recognition. Was this the man who'd paid her to hack Brett's security system? He didn't seem the type. He looked skittish and his clothes didn't seem to indicate he had the money to pull this scheme together.

"By his own admission, he came to see Whitney in person, believing they had a connection. He tried to talk to her while she was signing autographs outside the hotel but when she didn't acknowledge him, he grew angry and lashed out at her."

"That sounds like an impulsive act."

"It was. He claims he never meant to harm her. Unfortunately for Whitney, she hired you to protect her."

Jaycee noticed Brett's jaw clench as he held his temper. "It just so happens that we have proof that someone hired Jaycee here to hack into my security systems and take it offline. That wasn't the act of an impulsive person. That was premeditation. The real killer planned all of this."

Detective Hennessy rubbed his jaw. "What's this proof you claim to have?"

Jaycee handed him a copy of the invoice she'd found on her computer system. "I was hired to hack into B&W Security the night Whitney was killed and try to get around one of their systems. In my job, I test systems, and I was led to believe that's what I was doing, but when I saw what happened, I knew I'd been tricked."

"Who hired you?"

"I don't know his real name. He gave a fake name and blackmailed another client into giving me a recommendation so I would take him on as a client." She handed over a photograph of the man from the bank security feeds. Jackson had emailed a still image of him from the video and Brett and Jaycee had stopped to print it out on their way here. "This is him." And even Jaycee could see the man he had in custody couldn't be the man from the bank's video cameras. Their suspect was much taller and filled out. Lincoln Albertson was slender and looked like a stiff breeze might knock him over.

Hennessy was still skeptical. "What reason did he give you for wanting this done? Who did he claim to be?"

She felt her face flush. "I don't know. Someone tried

to kill me when I reached out to Brett to let him know what had happened. I was attacked in my apartment then again in my hotel room in Jessup. I crashed my car trying to escape from him and have no memory of what happened. Pieces of my memory have returned, but not all of it. Whoever this man is, he probably killed Whitney, and he tried to kill me too."

"My cousin has the police report about the incident in Jessup," Brett told the detective. "I can have him email you a copy."

"You do that. I'll see what I can find out about this guy in the photo but, until I do, we're keeping Mr. Albertson and charging him based on his confession. It's possible you opened the door for him by lowering the security system and he walked right in. It's also possible this all has nothing to do with Whitney's murder. We've got a solid case with a confession. It'll take a lot to prove to me that that confession is false."

Detective Hennessy led them to the exit and showed them out.

As they were climbing back into Brett's car, Jaycee realized the detective might have inadvertently revealed something important.

"What if whoever it was that hired me, wasn't intending on killing Whitney? Maybe Albertson saw his opportunity and took it, but that was never the plan."

"Then what was the plan?"

"To get back at you. Or at your company. Whitney might not have been the target at all. Maybe it was you. He could have wanted to humiliate you or your agency by proving you couldn't protect Whitney."

Brett's face reddened. "Mission succeeded."

"I'm just thinking that if the plan was to kill Whitney, then why let someone else do it? Why allow this Lincoln Albertson guy to get so close? Was it a fluke that he beat the real killer there? Or did it happen because the real perpetrator wasn't expecting it?"

He seemed to mull that thought over for a moment. "You might be onto something. One thing I'm certain of is that Albertson wasn't sophisticated enough to pull off this elaborate scheme."

"Plus, he wasn't the man in the images at the bank who blackmailed Jackson. He was way too short and slender."

"Jackson could have been lying about that to protect him. Or to protect himself."

"I don't believe he was lying." He'd seemed sincere, only now she wondered if she would even know sincerity or not. She bit her lip. "I don't know what to think."

"Let's head back to my office," Brett suggested. "Maybe you can pull more information from your system given more time. We'll also start the investigation into both of these men."

She nodded. That was a good idea. She'd only scratched the surface of her recovered hard drive and, now that she knew she wasn't a criminal, she was hoping she would be able to recover more. Maybe something in her files would give her some clarity about her involvement in all of this.

Someone had made her an accomplice to murder. She was determined to find out who.

They returned to the office and Jaycee spent the next few hours in the conference room searching through her drive's data, trying to reconstruct her files. It was slow going and she was only finding pieces of information with little context around them. After a few hours, she pushed back her chair and stood. She rolled her neck to work out the kinks.

It seemed like an enormous task. And a futile one. She wasn't uncovering the information she needed. She sighed. The truth was that what she needed wasn't stored in her computer files. It was locked inside her memories.

If only she could remember the man who'd hired her.

She glanced at the emailed image taken from the video surveillance that she had saved to her laptop. If only she could make out this man's face. All of her efforts to use facial recognition software to identify him had failed. There simply wasn't enough of his face visible to make it work. Maybe if she could look at the surveillance video again, she could find some angle that might work with facial recognition.

They'd only looked at a few minutes of the video at the bank then Brett had placed it into the console of his car. It was probably still there. It might yield nothing but it was better than what she was doing now.

She hurried out of the conference room and down the hall to his office. He wasn't there so she asked Trish at the receptionist desk if she knew where he was.

"He's in Wilson's office. They're trying to figure out a way to get the press to back off. They asked not to be disturbed. Can whatever you need wait?"

She sighed. "It'll have to, I guess. I was hoping to get his keys. There's a flash drive we left in his car that I wanted to get."

Trish smiled. "Well, I can help you with that." She opened a drawer and fished out a set of keys. "I have a spare to every lock in this building and ones to all the cars just in case. Here you go."

She took the keys from Trish, glad for their backup system. "That's great. Thanks. I'll be right back." She doubted Brett would even miss her. She would probably be sitting in the conference room before he was finished with his meeting.

After riding the elevator down to the garage, Jaycee hurried toward his Charger. Something stopped her. She glanced around, feeling like someone was watching her. She shook it off. She was safe here. Still, the sooner she retrieved that flash drive, the sooner she could return upstairs.

She headed to the car, unlocked the door then leaned in over the seat to look inside the console. She found the flash drive right where Brett had left it. Hopefully, it would provide some answers. They needed them.

As she backed out of the car, someone suddenly came up behind her and grabbed her, slamming something hard onto the back of her head. She slumped into the seat and someone pushed her legs inside and slammed the car door. Pain washed over her and darkness threatened to pull her down. She was helpless to stop it. She couldn't even cry out.

The last thing she heard before the blackness engulfed her was the sound of footsteps moving away.

# FIVE

Jaycee awoke with a start. Her head was pounding but she was still sitting in the driver's seat of Brett's Charger. She glanced around at the now-empty parking garage. Whoever had hit her was nowhere in sight.

The flash drive lay on the floor at her feet and she reached down to grab it. At least he hadn't gotten his hands on this. Her attacker's identity was ever more important now that he'd brazenly attacked her here at Brett's office.

Brett. She needed to tell him what had happened. B&W had security video. They could review that and possibly get an even better image of her assailant than what was on the flash drive.

She reached for the handle and pushed on the door, but it wouldn't move. She tried again and then manually checked the locks. It wasn't locked yet the door still wouldn't open. She leaned over to the passenger's side and tried that door. It wouldn't open either.

She was trapped inside a locked car with the engine running.

What was the point of this?

A moment later, she knew as exhaust fumes filled the interior of the car. She coughed then gagged then tried to shut off the engine, but pressing the button didn't work. She tried to open a window but they didn't lower.

She glanced around, hoping for Brett or someone to be walking past and help her. No one was there. That didn't stop her from banging on the window and calling out for help.

She used her jacket to cover her face and nose. The fumes were starting to make her light-headed. She pounded on the window again. Why hadn't she brought a phone or had someone come with her just in case? Because she hadn't planned on being ambushed in the parking garage, that's why.

She leaned across the seat and opened the glove box. Maybe something inside there could help her. What she wouldn't give for an extra cell phone or communication device or even something to break the window with. She dug through the compartment, tossing out napkins and the owner's manual. Nothing that would help her escape.

Her eyes stung from the fumes and she felt woozy. She had to alert someone to her presence if she had any chance of making it out of this alive. But how? She struggled to keep her eyes open, knowing if she closed them, that would be giving up and she wouldn't make it. But she couldn't panic either. That used up too much oxygen and there wasn't much of that left.

Then it hit her. If she couldn't call out, maybe she could get someone's attention another way.

She pressed on the horn and it blared. She pressed

it again and again. Hopefully, someone would hear it and come to her aid.

She wouldn't give up. She wouldn't let this maniac win. Only, she was getting weaker and weaker with each second that passed.

It wouldn't be long for her.

Brett walked past the empty conference room.

Jaycee wasn't there.

He checked the kitchen and several offices, but she was nowhere around. Odd. Where could she have gone without telling him?

He walked to the front desk. It, too, was empty.

Where had everyone gone?

He hurried down the hall, back to Wilson's office, and poked his head in the doorway. "Have you seen Jaycee? I can't find her. Trish is MIA too."

He stood, shaking his head. "Trish left for a doctor's appointment. She sent me an email. I haven't seen Jaycee."

"I'm worried. She wouldn't go off by herself."

"We'll find her." He patted Brett's shoulder as he rushed past. Brett quickly followed behind him. Wilson ran toward the front offices so Brett went in the opposite direction. He checked each office on the floor but didn't see her. He poked his head into one office and saw Mitch Dearborn, their newest security specialist, at his computer. "Hey, Mitch, I'm looking for a woman I brought in with me. Have you seen anyone wandering around?"

He shook his head and stood, just as Wilson had. "I haven't. Need some help searching?"

He nodded and took a deep breath. If she wasn't in trouble, she should have showed up by now. "I'd appreciate it."

He and Wilson gathered three other operatives who worked for the firm and they searched every room in the suite and the storage room in the vestibule. Now Brett was really worried.

He headed for the conference room. Maybe something there would alert him to where she'd gone. Irritation bit through him. She should know better than to go off on her own. Especially after being attacked multiple times.

Nothing stood out to him at first, but then he spotted the photograph from the bank of the man who called himself Joe Cleveland. He remembered the flash drive in the car. Maybe she'd gone down to get it.

Wilson appeared in the doorway of the conference room. "Brett, come see this."

He hurried to the security office where Mitch was pulling up the camera feeds. "We tracked her into the hallway and down to the parking garage, but look at this. The camera in the garage has been disabled."

That wasn't good. Panic filled him as he darted from the office and down the stairs to the parking garage, vaguely aware that Wilson and the others were behind him. He spotted his car and his heart stopped. Jaycee was slumped over the steering wheel and she wasn't moving. He ran to the car and tried to open the door.

It didn't budge.

Wilson tried the passenger's-side door. "It won't open. Looks like someone jammed it."

Brett looked at the door. He was right. Someone had used a nail gun to intentionally bolt the doors.

He pounded on the window, trying to wake her, but now that he was closer, he could see white smoke filling the car. He circled the car and saw a hose attached to the exhaust pipe. It was obviously pumping carbon monoxide into the car and he had no idea how long she'd been in there.

He ripped out the hose then ran and grabbed a fire extinguisher off the wall. He moved to the passenger's-side window and shattered the glass. He quickly slid inside, grabbed her arm and pulled her from the car. Wilson helped him lower her to the ground.

Brett leaned over her. She was pale and her lips were blue. "Jaycee? Stay with me, Jaycee."

"Call an ambulance," Wilson shouted at Mitch. "Brett, is she breathing?"

He checked for a pulse. It was faint. Fear rushed through him. He couldn't lose another one. He shook his head. "I—I don't think so."

Wilson pushed him aside. "I'm starting CPR."

Brett moved away while Wilson and Dave Boatner, another operative, worked on her until the ambulance arrived. The EMTs gave her oxygen and her color and breathing quickly improved.

"We'll need to transfer her to the hospital for a more thorough evaluation," one of the paramedics stated as they loaded her into the ambulance.

Brett nodded. "I'll be right behind you." He caught a glimpse through the window of a still-unconscious Jaycee on the stretcher as they sped away, and his heart clenched.

She'd been here at his office. She should have been safe here.

Mitch approached him. "It looks like your car was rigged to pump exhaust fumes back inside it. The starter button was jammed and the window fuses were removed so they wouldn't lower. The door jamming prevented her from getting out."

Brett pushed a hand through his hair. He understood Mitch's meaning. In addition to all that, the security camera had been disabled, so there would be no image of who'd done this. This hadn't been an accident. Someone had been watching and waiting for Jaycee, or possibly for both him and Jaycee to get into the car.

This had been an attempt on her life and it had been deliberate.

Brett paced the hallway at the hospital as he waited for news on Jaycee. He couldn't believe this had happened again. And on his watch. He dragged his fingers through his already disheveled hair.

His world felt like it was ending all over again. He'd already lost Whitney. Already let someone sneak past him and get to her. He couldn't allow that to happen again. He'd promised to keep Jaycee safe, but he was failing her. The killer had nearly gotten to her today.

*God, why is this happening again?*

He'd thought he was good at his job. He'd thought security was what he was meant to do, yet this situation, along with Whitney's murder, had him questioning everything.

But he wasn't going to let this incident stop him from

doing his best to protect Jaycee. He trusted Wilson and his team to investigate the scene and figure out what had happened and how the attacker had gotten so close. He would follow up with them once he knew Jaycee was going to be okay. He prayed they'd gotten to her in time.

"Brett." He glanced up to see his cousin Caleb hurrying his way.

"What are you doing here?"

"I was in town visiting Tucker, trying to get him to come to the ranch."

Their cousin Tucker was the fourth heir named in their grandfather's will. Brett hadn't seen him in years but had heard he was working SWAT for Dallas PD.

"I caught the call over the police scanner and recognized the name. How is Jaycee?"

"I don't know yet but she was unconsciousness when I found her."

He placed his hand on Brett's shoulder. "I'm sure she'll be okay. Any idea who did this?"

He shook his head. "I left Wilson and members of my team to investigate the scene while I came here. The police are there, too, making a report. I haven't heard back from them yet, but it looks like the security camera was disabled, the car doors and the ignition were jammed and the exhaust was rigged to pump carbon monoxide into the vehicle. Someone did this intentionally."

"Have you two found any evidence of who's behind these attacks or who killed Whitney?"

"We discovered that a man using the name Joe Cleveland paid Jaycee to hack into my company's security systems the night Whitney died, under the guise of testing the systems, but we're no closer to finding out who this guy is than we were when we started. We have a photograph and some video images but they haven't been useful in identifying him."

"Maybe Luke can help. He still has some contacts at the FBI."

Brett nodded. He'd thought about reaching out to Luke too. "Yeah, that's a good idea. I'll email it to him."

"Is there anything I can do?"

"I don't think so, Caleb, but thank you."

"I have someone at my office working on that other thing you asked me about," Caleb told him.

Brett shook his head, finding it hard to believe he could have doubted her. "I'm not sure that even matters now."

"Why don't you bring Jaycee back to the ranch? Between me, you and Luke, we can keep her safe there."

"I appreciate the thought but we need to be here to figure out who is doing this to her. We're not going to find the answers back at the ranch."

Caleb nodded. "Okay, but keep us in the loop. We'll be here for you if you need us. And the offer stands."

"I'm sure Luke wouldn't appreciate me bringing someone with a target on her head around his family."

Caleb looked serious. "He knows what it's like to have someone he cares about in trouble. He wouldn't blink at helping you and Jaycee. You don't know him like I do."

In fact, he hardly knew his cousins at all. They'd been practically kids the last time they'd all been together. Their fathers' deaths over only a few years' time had fractured the extended family, leaving their grandfather bitter and resentful, and the cousins scattered. He knew Tucker lived in Dallas, and Luke used to work there, too, until he'd retired. They'd all been so physically close together but had no connections other than blood.

The double doors opened and a nurse stuck her head through. "Mr. Harmon? She's asking for you."

"I'll call and check on you later," Caleb said.

He thanked his cousin then hurried after the nurse to a room down the hall.

Jaycee sat up in the bed. Her color looked better and she seemed bright and alert. He was certain the mask and oxygen pumping through her had had something to do with it. "How are you feeling?"

She lowered the mask to speak with him. "Much better."

Now that he knew she was okay, his mind turned to practical matters, the fading marks around her neck a reminder that this wasn't the first time this maniac had come after her. "Did you see who did this to you?"

She shook her head. "No, I didn't see anyone. I was looking for the flash drive. Someone hit me from behind, then I woke up to the car filling with fumes. I was so scared."

He squeezed her hand then reached out and stroked her cheek. He couldn't believe he'd nearly lost her.

Another thing he couldn't believe was how attached he'd become to her. He was depending on Jaycee and whatever was locked inside her brain to help him return his life to normal.

"I hate to ask, but have you remembered anything else about the man who hired you?"

She rubbed the back of her head. "You'd think getting hit in the head again might have shaken something loose, but nothing concrete. All my memories are coming back with pieces missing. My brain is like Swiss cheese."

He was disappointed but mostly he was glad she hadn't been injured any worse than she had been. "My cousin Caleb stopped by. He suggested we go back to Jessup, to the ranch. He and my cousin Luke could help protect you. What do you think?"

She shook her head. "I'm not ready to do that. We might need to be in Dallas."

"That's what I told him but I wanted to give you the option. I don't want anything like this to happen to you again."

She leaned back against the pillow. "I shouldn't have gone off alone. I should have known he would be watching. He's been too clever not to know we were at your office."

Of course, he would know they'd gone to his office. Had the killer been sitting and waiting, plotting his next shot at her? Or at them both? He had to have been.

"We have to find this guy. It's time we go on the offensive."

"How?"

"Once you're able, I want to start with Whitney's murder and work backward. It's pretty clear the guy Detective Hennessy has in custody didn't attack you today. I don't even know if he killed Whitney or not, but someone else is behind this. Someone else, our mysterious Joe Cleveland, is trying to tie up his loose ends. You're not safe until we find him."

She clutched his hand and he enjoyed the softness of her skin. *Keep it together, Harmon.* He couldn't allow himself to get distracted again. He wouldn't risk her life like that again.

She pushed back the blanket and tried to get out of bed. "I feel fine. I'm ready when you are."

"Hold on, Jaycee. That's the pure oxygen talking. Your body needs time to rest and recuperate. You've been through something traumatic."

"And I'm ready to find out who's behind it."

He urged her onto the bed and pulled the blanket over her then replaced the mask. Right now, it was the best thing for her lungs. "And we will. But first, get some rest. Let your lungs pump out all that CO you inhaled."

She grabbed his arm and pulled down the oxygen mask. "Will you stay with me?"

The last time he'd left her in a hospital room, she'd been attacked. That wasn't going to happen again. "I will."

She relaxed and fell back onto the bed. It wasn't long before her eyelids grew heavy and sleep overtook her again.

It would take some time for Jaycee to regain her strength and he wasn't leaving her side until she did.

He glanced at the small sofa that would be his bed tonight. It wouldn't be comfortable but comfort wasn't his goal. She would be safe then, tomorrow, they would do their best to figure out what was going on.

Despite a lingering headache and a sore throat, Jaycee felt better. After being released from the hospital the next morning, she was ready to figure out who was doing this to her. If her memories wouldn't return and her files weren't any further help, she would just have to figure it out by herself.

Well, not by herself. With Brett's help.

He'd stayed by her side all night, sleeping on that uncomfortable couch, and he was moving slower this morning, working out the kinks in his back. She should feel bad about making him sleep in such an uncomfortable position but she didn't. She'd felt safe with him around. Plus, she was sure he hadn't gotten much sleep anyway. He'd been on high alert for her safety.

He led her outside to a black SUV, shrugging when she gave him a questioning look. "It's a rental. I asked Wilson to deliver it along with your laptop." Of course, he couldn't use his Charger. It had been damaged and was probably either being held for evidence or at the body shop being repaired.

"Where are we headed?" she asked him once they'd both climbed inside. He'd said he wanted to start this investigation from Whitney's murder and work his way backward, but she wasn't certain what he'd meant by that.

"I thought we'd go to the hotel where Whitney was killed. The room is technically still a crime scene, but I talked to Detective Hennessy this morning and he said they're getting ready to release it. They've photographed, videoed, scanned and sampled every inch of it. He gave us the okay to examine it."

It made sense to start there. That was where everything had gone wrong. She'd tapped into their security system and someone had used that opening to murder Whitney Warren.

She shuddered, still shaken by her part in Whitney's death. She believed she'd been tricked by Joe Cleveland, but that didn't change anything. A woman was still dead. And Brett's reputation was still in shambles. She couldn't turn a blind eye to her part in all of this.

They drove to the hotel and Brett grabbed the computer bag, which held her laptop. They stopped briefly to speak with someone he knew in security, who provided them the room key and promised to email him the hotel's security videos from the night Whitney was murdered.

Then, they went upstairs to the eighth-floor hotel room. Crime scene tape still hung across the door in an X shape. He pulled the tape away and opened the door.

A musty smell hit her as she stepped forward. This room had been sealed for weeks.

She saw Brett's jaw tense as they walked inside. There was a large couch and two chairs in front of a fireplace, a bar area with a kitchenette, and a separate bedroom.

She noticed an alarm panel on the wall and walked over to it, instinctively knowing everything about how it operated. Her Swiss-cheesed brain struck again. "It's a Delta 582 model. One of the best on the market."

"That's right. This room is one of a few that has a panel that allows security details to tap into the hotel's wiring without having to drill holes in the walls. A lot of good it did," Brett said, allowing a hint of resentment to seep into his tone.

She turned to him and felt her face flush. It might be the best on the market but she was obviously the best at getting through systems.

"No system is foolproof," she reminded him. "There's always a way around. You just have to know where to look. That's why human security is so important. A computer, even a little computer like this alarm, can't make choices and decisions. It has to be told what to do and when to do it. Those things can be manipulated."

"Is that how you did it, by manipulating them?"

Her face reddened again and she shrugged. "I might have told the alarm to shut down but to leave the lights on so it looked like it was working correctly." She'd nonchalantly changed his security settings and a woman had been killed. She hadn't done it with any malice on her part. She thought she'd been doing a job and she'd done it well. Too well.

"Who set up this security system for you? Did you do it yourself or outsource it?"

"We have a part-time consultant named Sean Knight. I tried to contact him after Whitney was murdered, but he'd left the country on a missionary trip."

She might need to check the security feeds herself to make sure he'd added enough protections. However many he had, though, had been no match for her skills.

"You still don't remember who hired you?"

"No." She closed her eyes and tried to imagine him. "I can almost see the man sitting across from me, but I can't make out his face. I remember feeling very comfortable with him though. He wasn't threatening at the time." Then she remembered crouching under her desk as shots fired into her apartment building. She shuddered at the sudden memory. "I'm sure he was much different when he tracked me down at my apartment to murder me."

"You shouldn't make jokes like that." He walked over to the center of the room. "She died right here. The killer jimmied the lock, pushed his way inside and had probably shot her before she'd even realized what had happened."

He'd heard her cry for help and come running from his room next door.

"How did he get past the security latch on the door?" She noticed it was still intact.

He shrugged. "It's easy enough to find a video on the internet to show you how to do that." He rubbed his hand over the back of his neck. "She just wanted some time to herself. She was still really grieving over the death of her fiancé. She never got over him. She loved Tony a lot, but this acting thing kind of took off for her only a few months after he died. She took the job because she wanted to stay busy so she didn't dwell on her grief. Only, the show she was hired to do became a hit and suddenly her image was all over the place. She was an instant star and she didn't have the time to wallow in her loss.

"She contacted our firm four months ago. Said she'd been getting threatening phone calls and letters. She chose our firm because of our connection to Tony. I traveled with her for several months then, when she wanted to return to Dallas, I chose this hotel. I thought she would be safe here. I was right next door. The shooter was already running away when I got here but Whitney needed my attention. By the time I realized it was too late for her, he was gone. I still don't understand how I let this happen."

"It's not your fault, Brett."

"I should have seen it though. I'm trained to see things like this. I promised her I would keep her safe. I couldn't do that."

"It wasn't your fault, Brett. If anyone here is at fault, it's me. I practically opened the door for the man. I should have known he wasn't on the up-and-up. I missed it. How many others did I miss without realizing it?" Suddenly, the idea of getting all her memories back and knowing that number didn't sound so hot.

She removed her laptop and connected to the security alarm and downloaded the files and processes so she could better understand the techniques she'd used to get around the system.

It wouldn't bring Whitney back but at least she could help Brett and Wilson guard against anything like this—anyone like her—breaching their systems again.

They returned to B&W Security where Jaycee was greeted by Trish, Wilson and several other operatives she hadn't previously met. They all told her how glad they were that she was okay. But she wasn't okay. At least, not mentally. She'd let down her guard and the man who was after her had nearly killed her.

She had to remain on alert if she had any hope of getting out of this nightmare alive.

She settled back into the conference room then ran through the information she'd downloaded from the alarm system in the hotel room. As she'd suspected, she'd manipulated the program to set it to sleep mode. Useful information but not something that was going to help them figure out who was behind these attacks.

Jaycee pulled up the list Brett had sent her of the people Whitney had thought might be after her. They'd decided to have her go through each name one by one. They both agreed Lincoln Albertson was unlikely to be behind the conspiracy they'd uncovered. Jaycee still couldn't picture the man who'd hired her, but she was more certain than ever it hadn't been Albertson.

Besides, he'd been in jail when the last attack on her had occurred. That meant he couldn't have been involved, at least, not on his own.

Either he was a patsy, like she was, or else he was a scapegoat.

Regardless, he was on the list of people who'd targeted Whitney. Letters she'd received had been traced back to him. Brett had made copies of them when she'd first hired him and they were on the company's server. Of course, Whitney hadn't known they'd come from Albertson when she'd hired Brett. Jaycee pulled them up and read through them. They'd started out innocently enough with Albertson writing how much he liked her and wanted to meet her. They'd escalated from there, eventually getting to the obsessive, stalker variety. If Jaycee wasn't aware of Joe Cleveland and his involvement, it might be easy to believe that Albertson had broken into the hotel and shot Whitney like the obsessed fan he appeared to be based on these letters.

She pulled up his social media history. That was just

as disturbing as his letters had been. Multiple posts about Whitney and their so-called relationship. He'd even posted about flying to Dallas to meet with her at the hotel.

Jaycee retrieved his financial records and skimmed through them. She saw no charges for a plane ticket from his home in Florida to Dallas.

Interesting.

She went to the camera feeds the hotel manager had given Brett and double-checked the images. She spotted Albertson mingling with a crowd across the street from the hotel the day Whitney had been murdered. He'd definitely been there. No wonder the police believed they had their man.

But how had he gotten there?

She wished she had access to the airlines to find out who had paid for Albertson's plane ticket to Dallas. That would certainly give them some idea who was behind this. She could probably hack into the airline system but without knowing which airline he'd taken and when, it would be a futile search.

She would talk with Brett about how to find out that information. Maybe they could speak with Albertson or his lawyer. She also wanted to see the hotel's interior security feeds. If Albertson had gotten inside to Whitney, those would show it.

She made a note on the paper then moved on to the next person on the list. A rival actress Whitney had beat out for a movie role. The woman had screamed at Whitney as she'd walked to her car and threatened to get her revenge. Could that revenge include murder?

Jaycee pored through every online detail she could find. She found no threats of violence, criminal records or social media posts that indicated she was involved in Whitney's murder. The actress was clean, as were the next five people on Whitney's list, as far as Jaycee could tell.

She pushed back from the conference room table and stood, stretching. It was tedious work but necessary if they wanted to find out who had targeted Whitney. Whoever it was had pulled Jaycee into his plan as well.

Trish knocked then stuck her head inside. "Lunch is here." She handed Jaycee a box with a sandwich, chips and a bottled fruit drink. "I hope you enjoy it."

Brett had insisted she not leave the office, so she'd been relegated to getting her lunch delivered.

"Thanks. Is Brett having lunch too?"

"Sure. I ordered for the whole team. They're having a meeting in the back hall. Trying to work out some solutions for getting new clients. I'm afraid this mess with Whitney Warren has hurt us reputation-wise."

"I know. I hate the part I played in this. I'm hoping to help uncover something to prove who was really behind her murder. The answer has to be on this list. Someone with the money and the sophistication to plan this out was targeting Whitney. I'm hoping I can find out who and why."

Trish gave her a sympathetic look. "I'm sure you're doing everything you can. I can tell Brett really trusts you."

"He does?" She flushed at the way her comment sounded. Like a schoolgirl discovering that a boy liked her. She wasn't blind to Brett's attractiveness but it felt pointless to even think about such things. She'd been the cause of him losing a client.

He might trust her. He might even acknowledge that she wasn't to blame. But he would never be able to forget it.

Trish nodded. "He and Whitney had gotten very close during their time together. She meant a lot to him, so it was extra difficult to lose her. She used to be engaged to one of Brett and Wilson's teammates, you know."

"I had heard that," Jaycee said. "I know they were close. I want to find the person responsible for her death just as much as he does." It would mean a lot to her to help find justice for Whitney. It would be like a redemption. Plus, then the killer would stop targeting her too.

"I'd better get back and deliver everyone else's food," Trish stated. "Enjoy your lunch."

Jaycee sat back down and bit into her sandwich and chips. They were good but salty, so she was glad for the drink. She'd hoped to have lunch with Brett but it seemed that wasn't to be. The man sure took a lot of meetings. She reminded herself to stop complaining. She wasn't there for lunch. She was there to work and figure this out. Brett was doing his part. It was time she did hers too.

She pushed the food away and turned back to the list. She still had a ways to go.

The next name on Whitney's list was Jack Milton, a producer Whitney had worked with on her television show. She hadn't gone into specifics about why she'd included him on the list, so Jaycee looked him up on the internet. He was definitely sleazy. She found multiple accusations of him trading roles for sexual favors. There were even accusations of sexual assault, but no charges or convictions on his record.

Was it possible Whitney had been involved with this producer? One of his victims perhaps? She needed to talk with Brett about it.

Jaycee's vision blurred and her eyes felt heavy. A headache pressed down on her. Probably from staring at this screen for so long.

She stood and suddenly felt ill. The room began to tilt and nausea rolled through her.

Something was wrong. This wasn't just being tired from too much work. It felt different than that and it had hit her too fast.

She turned to reach for the cell phone Brett had given her as a precaution, but her hand slipped and knocked it against her beverage, spilling the remaining contents onto the table. She needed to clean that up before it reached her computer, but she couldn't make her body move fast enough.

She tried to pick up the cell phone again and only managed to slide it to the floor. She crawled down to get it. She couldn't make her fingers grip it, so she just pushed the buttons, hitting the speed dial that rang directly to Brett.

He was cheerful as he answered. "Hi, Jaycee, how's it going?"

"Help me," she groaned. "Something...something's wrong."

His voice changed instantly. "I'm on my way."

She heard footsteps and shouting heading toward the conference room, then the door burst open and Brett's panicked voice rang out.

"Jaycee!" He hurried to her and rolled her over so that she was looking up at him. The worry on his face was evident. "Jaycee, stay with me."

"I don't… I don't feel good." Her voice was low and her words slurred. "Something's wrong."

"Did something happen? Did someone hurt you?"

She tried to say that no, nothing had happened, but the headache pressed down on her.

"What happened?" A male voice asked the question. Jaycee glanced up to see Wilson and Trish standing in the doorway, several people behind them.

"I don't know," Brett responded. "Call an ambulance. I don't see any injuries but something isn't right with her." Brett touched her face as he urged her to stay with him. "Jaycee, look at me. Stay awake. Can you tell me what happened?"

Her eyelids were so heavy…

Her last thought before the darkness pulled her under was how much she enjoyed being in his arms.

The paramedic rushed into the room and moved Brett aside as his partner pushed a gurney to the doorway of the conference room. "What happened here?"

Brett did his best to get out of their way but he felt helpless seeing her lying on the floor. "I'm not sure. She called me and said something was wrong. By the time I got here from down the hall, she was on the floor. Said she felt sick, and her words were slurring."

"I don't see any obvious wounds. Was she alone?"

"As far as I know." Brett looked at Trish, who nodded.

"She was in here alone the last time I saw her."

"Did she ingest anything?"

Trish stepped into the room. "I brought her lunch we ordered from that sandwich shop down the road. Turkey sandwich, chips and a drink. But the entire office ate from there and no one else is sick."

The paramedic nodded and glanced at the uneaten food left on the table. "Still, let's bag this up. I'll drop it by the lab just to be sure, but the emergency room will run tests to determine what might have happened. Does she have a history of seizures?"

"Not that I'm aware of but she's got some memory loss." Brett quickly bagged up what remained of her lunch and handed it to the paramedic.

The paramedics loaded Jaycee onto a gurney and headed to the hospital. Brett wanted nothing more than to be with her, but first, he had to try to figure out what had happened here. She'd been fine the last time he'd seen her before lunch so something must have happened to her during that time.

He glanced around the conference room. The only signs of a struggle he saw was the overturned drink. Was it possible someone had poisoned her food or drink? He'd sent the food with the paramedic but not the drink bottle. He used a napkin to pick it up and place it into a bag. The bottle was nearly empty, the remainder of its contents covering the table.

Wilson picked up a roll of paper towels and started to clean it up. "Do you want to take these too?"

He shook his head. "It's the same stuff. They can test the bottle."

"What about the computer stuff? Do you want to take it to your office for safekeeping?"

He could hardly think about that and was glad Wilson had suggested it, but it wasn't necessary. "We'll just lock the conference room door. No one should be in or out of here."

Wilson nodded then tossed the paper towels into a wastebasket. "Do you want me to drive you to the ER?"

"No, I'll be fine." He was shaking inside though doing his best to keep it together. He couldn't believe another attack had occurred. Here in their offices where she definitely should have been safe.

He couldn't even digest yet what that meant.

He locked the conference room door and instructed Trish that no one should enter it. If someone had spiked Jaycee's food, that made their conference room a crime scene.

He prayed that wasn't the case. The paramedic had alluded to seizures. For all he knew, she had them and this was nothing more than a medical event. They hadn't found any medication in her apartment to indicate she had any type of condition but it was always possible she carried them in a purse. She hadn't had one when he'd first found her and they hadn't located one in the hotel either. In fact, her identification and credit cards—that she'd definitely had when checking into the hotel since they'd made a copy of them—were nowhere to be found. Whoever had attacked her must have taken everything with him.

And given the previous pattern of attacks against her, what was the likelihood that this was a simple medical event?

Although now that they knew her name, the emergency room personnel could check their records for any medical history. Since she lived in Dallas, she probably would have had medical treatment somewhere and it might be in the systems. There were only two major hospitals in the area. If she wasn't in one, she had to be in the other.

He drove to the hospital and explained to the check-in nurse about the drink bottle. She took it from him and promised to pass it along. She told him to have a seat and she would alert someone to his presence.

Time seemed to stand still but his mind kept replaying the events over and over. No matter how hard he tried, he couldn't make himself believe this was a simple seizure. Something was going to come back on those test results. He was sure of it. Some unknown person had been targeting Jaycee since the night he'd met her.

This couldn't be a coincidence.

She should have been safe at the security offices, but she hadn't been. She'd been attacked twice there, and that baffled him more than anything. He couldn't even keep her safe in his own building. What chance did he have of keeping her safe anywhere?

He needed to get out of his head. He couldn't wrap his head around the fact that someone he knew, someone close to him, might be a killer.

"Mr. Harmon?" A man in scrubs called his name.

He stood. "I'm Brett Harmon."

The man motioned for Brett to follow him through the double doors and down a hallway. "Is she okay?" His heart ached at the thought that Jaycee might not be.

At a door, the doctor turned to him. "She's going to be fine. We ran some tests and found traces of antifreeze in her system. We've contacted the police to report this attempt on her life."

His heart sank into his gut. "Are you sure?"

"No doubt about it. The lab will test for trace evidence of the substance inside the bottle you brought in. Someone might have spiked her drink."

"Wouldn't she have tasted that?"

"The flavor could have masked it. I'm sure the police will want to ask you questions regardless."

He nodded. "I'm sure they will. Can I see her?"

The doctor gave in. "She's been asking for you. She insists you're not the one who did this to her and, since you brought the bottle in yourself, I'm giving you the benefit of the doubt, but leave the door open and I'm having security post a guard outside the room."

He nodded. "That's a good idea. Thank you, Doctor."

He walked into the room and saw Jaycee lying on the bed. She looked so frail even though he knew she wasn't. She was strong and determined. He swallowed hard, realizing how he'd failed her. He wouldn't let what happened to Whitney happen to her too.

He moved to the bedside then reached and took her hand. "How do you feel?"

"Better. Thanks for coming when I called."

He kissed her hand, surprised by the emotion sweeping through him. "Always."

She stared at him and despite how much he wanted to protect her from this, he could see she already knew the truth. The doctor had told him as much.

"The lab found traces of antifreeze in your drink."

She nodded. "I know. They told me." A single tear slipped down her cheek. "When is this going to stop? I just want this to stop."

He pulled her into his arms and hugged her. "I know. So do I. I think we need to leave town for a while, go back to Jessup. We can stay at my grandfather's ranch. You'll be safe there. No one will be able to get to you."

He felt her tense. "How do you know?"

"My cousin is the chief of police, remember? And my other cousin, Luke, is retired FBI. Between the three of us, we should be able to protect you."

"Are you sure you can trust them?"

Her question tugged at his heart. She knew what he'd also come to realize. They couldn't trust the people around them. "I hadn't seen them in a while before the other day, but I trust them. Caleb is the one who suggested it. I turned him down at first, but now I think it's a good choice for us." He hadn't been close to his cousins since childhood but he knew they were good men. Both Caleb and Luke had the investigative, enforcement and protection skills he needed to help keep her safe. It didn't hurt that neither of them had had any involvement with either Whitney or Jaycee. He touched her face as he locked eyes with hers. "We will keep you safe, Jaycee. I promise you."

She nodded. “Okay then.”

That was settled. They had questions to answer from the police and he needed to return to the office to gather her files and data from the conference room, then they would be on their way. He would do it himself instead of asking someone else to do it. He didn’t trust anyone in that office anymore.

His worst fear had been realized. Only someone inside his office could have spiked Jaycee’s drink. Only someone there would have known which meal was for her.

Someone inside his office was involved.

He no longer trusted anyone around him.

# SIX

Brett's jaw clenched as he drove under the sign announcing Harmon Ranch. They'd ended up spending the night at the hospital again and, after completing paperwork, answering the police's questions and undergoing multiple tests to make certain Jaycee's kidneys and other organs hadn't been affected, she'd gotten the okay to be released by 10:00 a.m. They'd been on the road to Jessup soon after.

He couldn't believe he was here again. He'd said he would never return and now he'd been back twice in the span of a week.

He used to love this place and the pull the land had on him, but that had been before his father had passed away and his grandfather had changed into a person he didn't like. Brett didn't know if the pain of losing all four of his sons had so broken his grandfather that he wasn't able to open himself up any longer or if he'd just allowed resentment and anger to rule his life. Either way, Brett's last memory of Harmon Ranch hadn't been a pleasant one. He'd said goodbye to this place where he'd spent his childhood and every summer vacation until his fourteenth birthday.

Now, he was using it as a refuge to hide someone he cared about from a killer.

He pulled up behind a couple of other cars and turned off the SUV. "We made it." He reached across the seat and took Jaycee's hand, enjoying the feel of her fingers wrapped in his. "You'll be safe here until we figure all this out."

"And you're sure your cousins are okay with this? I don't want to put anyone in danger."

"Yes, I spoke to Caleb and told him we were coming."

She nodded and stared up at him with those innocent dark eyes. He knew he would do everything to keep her safe.

The front door opened and Caleb, Luke, Abby, Dustin and Kenzie exited. Abby waved.

"Looks like the greeting squad is here," Brett joked. He felt Jaycee tense. "It's okay. You're safe here." He gave her hand a squeeze before they both got out. He walked around the vehicle and stood by her side as they greeted everyone.

Caleb walked off the porch to shake Brett's hand. "You made it. Good."

"We made good time," Brett said. Seeing five pairs of eyes staring at them was enough to make him uncomfortable, so he couldn't imagine how Jaycee was feeling. He noticed she'd inched closer to him as they'd approached the house.

Time for introductions. "Jaycee, you remember my cousin Caleb. He's the police chief in town."

She nodded. "It's nice to see you again."

"You too. You look better than the last time I saw you."

The bruises on her face and neck had faded a little, though she still looked pale in Brett's opinion. And why wouldn't she? She'd been attacked three more times since leaving Jessup.

He motioned toward the family on the porch. "That's my other cousin, Luke, and you remember Abby from the hospital?"

Abby smiled and nodded. "And these are our kids, Kenzie and Dustin." She pointed to a boy and a girl who both said hi as she called their name. "They're on a school break for the next few days."

Jaycee put on a brave front. "It's nice to meet you all. I appreciate your letting me come here."

Abby stepped off the porch and took Jaycee's arm. "Nonsense. You're welcome here. Now, I asked Hannah, the housekeeper, to make up a room for you. The yellow room. It has a private bath and a great view of the stables. Plus, it's right across the hall from Brett's old room."

He grabbed their belongings then followed Abby and Jaycee as they entered the house, thankful Luke's wife had such a welcoming nature. She was one person Jaycee still remembered and, as he recalled from her time at the hospital, she'd been kind to her. Now, she was doing her best to put Jaycee at ease.

"I like your wife a lot," he told Luke as he stepped onto the porch.

Luke grinned and shook his hand. "I like her too."

"Go on and get settled in. We'll be in the kitchen if you want to join us in a bit," Caleb told him.

He nodded his agreement as he hurried up the staircase after Jaycee and Abby.

Stepping back into this house was like stepping back into his childhood, but he pushed away those feelings of anger and resentment toward his grandfather. Chet Harmon was no longer here, yet, without his presence, the big house seemed empty. He headed down the hallway of bedrooms and pushed open the door to one of the guest rooms known to the family as the "yellow room" because it was decorated in yellow.

Jaycee stood at the window with Abby, who was pointing out the stables.

He set her things on the bed. "Everything okay?"

Abby turned and smiled. "Everything is fine." She looked at Jaycee for confirmation. To his relief, she smiled in return.

"Yes, everything is good."

"I'm making lunch if you'd like to come down and join us," Abby told them both.

Jaycee waved her off. "Thank you but it was a long drive and I'm still a little weak after all that's happened. I'd like to rest for a while."

"I understand. I'll check on you later then."

As she left the room, Brett dropped his bag on the floor and walked over to Jaycee. He stroked a strand of hair near her face and hated the weariness still evident in her eyes. "Are you sure you're okay?"

She nodded and stared up at him. "I'll be okay. I'm just tired. Long drive and all that. I think I just want to rest for a while. Is that okay?"

"Sure it is. Take all the time you need. You're safe

here, Jaycee. I won't let anything happen to you." From the moment he'd pulled her away from that wrecked car, she'd been a distraction then a means to figuring out who had killed Whitney, but something had changed. She was more than that to him now. Yes, he still wanted answers, but not at the risk of her life. And now that he suspected someone in his office was involved, he owed it to her to keep her safe. They needed one another.

"My room is across the hall."

She followed his gaze across the hall to a closed door then nodded. "I'll be fine," she reassured him.

He hoped so. "If you need anything, just knock. If I'm not there, I'll be downstairs. I won't go anywhere without letting you know first."

He grabbed his bag and walked across the hall, pushing open his old bedroom door. He watched her until she closed her door before stepping into his room. He tossed the bag onto his bed. He'd been back here only a few days ago to sleep, but little more. He hadn't had the time to really inspect it. Nothing, it seemed, had changed since he was a kid. Each of the grandkids had gotten their own bedrooms when they'd visited, but Brett remembered all four of them choosing to build a fort in the living room instead of sleeping apart whenever they were together.

They'd all been close once and, even though he couldn't say they were now, it meant a lot to have his cousins here when he needed them. They hadn't hesitated to help him or Jaycee.

He walked downstairs and found his cousins and Abby in the kitchen sitting around the table. He joined them, sliding into his old chair like he'd been there forever.

"How's she holding up?" Caleb asked as he settled in.

"She's scared, but she's tough. I think it'll be good for her to be here. At least I know she's out of the line of fire."

Abby handed him a plate full of pot roast, green beans and potatoes. It smelled delicious. "I'll take her plate up to her once we're finished here," she promised.

"Thank you," Brett said, looking up at her with gratitude. "I know she appreciates seeing a familiar face."

"I'm happy to do it." She glanced at her husband then smiled. "I know what it's like to have someone threaten everything you've worked for."

He remembered the story of how Abby had fought to find her daughter when Kenzie had been abducted by a human trafficking ring. She'd put her life on the line and come through on the other side.

That was the kind of strength Jaycee needed now.

Abby fixed the plate then exited the room, leaving Brett and his cousins alone.

"So what happened?" Luke asked once she was gone.

"Jaycee was attacked at my office. First time, in the parking garage. At first, I just figured whoever was after her had followed us there, but then someone spiked her drink with antifreeze. The only way they could have gotten to her was if it was someone inside the office and they knew which drink was hers. I had to get her out of there."

Caleb nodded. "You made the right decision bringing her here."

Luke leaned forward. "I reached out to my contact at the FBI. She tried running facial recognition from that photo that you gave me, but they weren't able to come up with anything. There weren't enough points on the face to come up with a good match."

Brett rubbed his hand through his hair. That's what he had been afraid of. Even having a photograph of the man who was responsible for all this had gotten them nowhere.

"Jaycee still hasn't remembered him?" Caleb asked.

He shook his head. "She's slowly getting some memories back, but so far nothing that has helped identify the man who hired her to hack into our systems the night Whitney was killed."

"If your office has been compromised, we need to figure out who it is. Have you had any new hires?"

He shook his head. "No. The last person we hired was Mitch Dearborn. He's a former army ranger. Been with us for six months. He's solid. He's done good work, according to Wilson."

Caleb raised an eyebrow. "According to Wilson? You mean, you don't know?"

He shrugged. "I was on the road with Whitney for much of that time, but I've seen Mitch's records and he's been a stand-up guy. The rest of the team has been with us for years. We hired Mitch because business was booming." They'd attributed their increased success to the PR Brett had gotten from being Whitney's bodyguard.

They could now also attribute their company's decline to that as well.

Caleb still had questions. "Have you recently had to let anyone go?"

He shook his head. "I don't think so, but Wilson handles most of the business stuff. He hasn't mentioned having to fire anyone recently or having trouble with any of our specialists." Except him, of course.

"You should still check in with him and find out. If someone in your office has been compromised, he needs to know about it."

His cousins were right. Brett needed to ask more questions of Wilson about the staff. He'd let Wilson take over that part of the business for too long. If he was right and it was someone in his office who'd spiked Jaycee's drink, Wilson needed to be on the lookout.

"I'll call him now." He pulled out his cell phone.

Caleb stood. "In the meantime, I'll let Ed know that we're locking down the ranch. We'll close the front gates. No one gets in or out without a reason." Ed Lance had managed Harmon Ranch for as long as Brett could recall. "Who all knows you're here?"

"Only Wilson and Trish, but they don't know why I decided to come here. I'm sure they just think it was because of yet another attack on Jaycee. They don't know I suspect someone in the office is involved."

"You need to go through your personnel records too," Luke suggested. "Maybe do another background check or financials on each of your employees. You might find someone who needed some extra cash and suddenly got it. Even if they weren't responsible for Whitney's death, maybe they were paid to get close and get to Jaycee."

He nodded and stood. That was a good idea. People

were often easy to manipulate when plagued with financial issues. Harry Jackson was proof enough of that… but he wasn't one of Brett's team. "Most of our employee files are online. Jaycee and I can go through them from here." It would not only benefit them, it would also give them something to do besides just sitting around waiting for another attack.

Luke touched his shoulder as he rose. "Don't worry, Brett. We'll do our best to keep her safe."

He thanked them both and watched them walk out. He was glad he'd brought Jaycee here. He knew his cousins didn't have anything to do with Whitney's death or the danger Jaycee was in.

They would help keep her safe until he could figure out who was targeting her.

Jaycee stared out the window that overlooked the stables. She smiled at the idea of horses and country living. Even though she was certain she'd never lived on a ranch, she liked the idea of so much open space.

Yet that only reminded her of someone out there lurking to find her and kill her.

She turned away from the window.

Abby had brought her a lunch plate, which sat mostly uneaten. How could she concentrate on food after what had just happened to her? She turned away from it despite the rumbling in her stomach.

One thing she knew for certain, she felt safer here at Harmon Ranch as evidenced by the four straight hours of restful sleep she'd just awoken from.

She knocked on Brett's door and, when he didn't

answer, she headed for the stairs to find him, hearing laughter floating up the staircase. She followed the voices and found Brett among the rest of the family seated at a round kitchen table.

Abby noticed her first and waved her into the room. "Jaycee, hi! Come on in."

Everyone else turned, and she felt her face warm at the sudden attention.

Kenzie stood. "Dustin and I were just going upstairs to play a videogame." She grabbed her brother's plate then placed them both into the sink before they hurried out.

Jaycee held her own plate. She carried it to the sink then turned to Abby. "Thank you for the lunch. It was good. I guess I just wasn't very hungry."

Abby smiled. "I understand. You've been through a lot. I didn't know what kind of food you liked to eat."

She felt her face flush. "I don't really know either."

Abby gave her a sympathetic smile. "Well, who doesn't like pot roast, am I right?" She laughed then led Jaycee toward the table.

Brett pulled out a chair for her and Jaycee sat down. "I feel like I'm interrupting a family meeting or something."

"Not at all," Brett assured her. "We were just catching up. Talking about old times growing up here on the ranch."

"Sounds nice."

All the men's smiles seemed to fade. Brett gave a thoughtful nod. "We had our good times, but my grandfather—this was his place—he was a hard man to be around."

"I'm sorry. I didn't know."

"He left each of us plus our other cousin, Tucker, a piece of the ranch when he died a few months ago. That's why we all came back here…except for Caleb, who never left."

"You grew up here?"

Caleb nodded. "My mother dropped me off here with my grandfather when I was twelve years old. My dad had died in a car accident and she was so busy working that she didn't have anyone to watch me. She left me here and never came back."

"That's terrible. Did you all grow up here?"

Brett shook his head. "We lived here when I was younger but after my father died, my mother and I moved away. Grandpa Chet was never really a part of my life except for a few summers spent here and birthday presents he sent."

"Consider yourself blessed then," Luke stated. "I grew up just a few miles away from here. Grandpa and my mom didn't get along, so what little time I spent on the ranch was tense. I loved the place, just not the person I was forced to see whenever I came here."

Brett leaned forward. "Our grandfather wasn't the best guy in the world although, oddly, I remember a time when he was different. I think losing all four of his sons, our fathers, took its toll on him. Unfortunately, he was too busy grieving his own losses to realize we'd lost them too."

"That's terrible."

Jaycee remembered her own empty apartment. She, too, was obviously alone in the world. At least these men all had one another. "Have you all remained close?"

They glanced at each another then Brett shook his head. "No, not really. I haven't seen either of these guys in over six years, and it's been almost a decade since I've seen Tucker."

They nodded in agreement.

"We all seemed to go our separate ways," Caleb agreed.

Luke interjected. "But we're together now. I never thought I'd be back here in Jessup, living on this ranch with a wife and kids, but here I am. God's plans aren't always our plans."

Brett shook his head. "I'm happy for you, but I don't see that happening for me. I have a business I hope to salvage. I have a life I enjoy in Dallas."

"Well, that doesn't mean you have to be a stranger," Caleb told him. "You're always welcome here, no matter what you decide to do with your share."

Luke nodded his agreement and Jaycee noticed Brett's reaction. He seemed touched to have his cousins reach out to him that way. She found it nice that he had a family who cared about him.

He looked at Jaycee then turned back to his cousins. "Thank you but, first, we have to figure out who is targeting Jaycee. Until we figure all that out, my life and Jaycee's life are on hold." Brett reached over and held her hand. "We'll figure it out. Don't worry."

She clutched his in response, glad she wasn't having to endure this alone. She'd been right to come to him, whatever her reasons.

"Do you feel up to taking a walk?" he asked her. "I'd love to show you the ranch before dark."

She nodded. “I feel fine now.” All the aches and cloudiness she’d experienced were gone. Physically, she felt revived and refreshed. “I’d love to take the tour.”

He led her outside and they walked down by the stables where she saw multiple horses in the pasture. “Your grandfather owned all of these? He must have loved horses.”

“Last I heard, he only owned three or four of his own. The rest belong to people he stables for, I think, although Luke and Caleb might own some too. The ranch foreman and ranch hands care for them. The people who work here have been with my grandfather for years. He might not have been able to keep up with his grandsons but he somehow engendered loyalty from the people who worked for him.” He grabbed her hand. “Come here, I want to show you something.”

He led her down another path that opened up into a field with a big pond. He picked up a handful of rocks and tossed them into the water, skipping them across the surface as he hurried onto an old wooden pier. “This used to be my favorite place to come when my dad brought me here. We fished off this pier together.”

“How old were you when he died?”

“I was nine. The last time we were here, just before he deployed for his last mission overseas, he and my grandfather and me and my cousins spent the afternoon fishing. It was a good day. My dad shipped out two weeks after that.” His jaw clenched at the memory. “He never came home. He was killed in action when an RPG hit his convoy.”

“I’m so sorry.”

"My mom remarried six months after he died. They knew one another from church and he had been friends with them both before my dad's death. Charlie is a good man. He was a good stepfather to me. He taught me a lot and I'm thankful I had him." His jaw clenched and he tossed another rock into the water. "My grandfather did not take her remarriage well. He said it was too soon, although now I think he would have never approved of it. He felt like she was betraying my dad by remarrying."

His tone held a hint of anger but more hurt than anything else. "I visited the ranch a few more times after that, but everything had changed. My grandfather was a different man. Losing my dad, on top of losing his other sons…well, he wasn't that man I remembered from that day we spent fishing. He let his grief overwhelm him, rule his life. All he could see was what he'd lost. He never accepted my stepdad and never forgave me for accepting him into my life either." He swallowed hard at the painful memory. "The last words he ever said to me were to tell me how disappointed my dad would have been at me. I was sixteen at the time and his words broke me."

"He shouldn't have said that." She was shocked that an adult could be so cruel. The urge to hug him was strong but she resisted and rested her hand on his shoulder instead as a show of support. "I'm sure your dad would have been very proud of you."

"Charlie told me the same thing. My mom died when I was a teenager. He was the one who encouraged me to follow in my dad's footsteps by joining the marines. He always believed in me. I'm fortunate to have him in my life. He moved to Florida a few years ago and, last time I spoke to him, he was dating a lady he met at the senior center. I'm happy for him. My mom would have wanted him to be happy again."

It was nice the way he talked about his family. He was surrounded by people who cared about him. It was a nice comparison to how empty her life seemed. According to her parents' obituary, she had no other family. Even if she remembered how much she'd cared for them, she would still be going back to a lonely apartment once this was over with.

He glanced at her and his cheeks reddened. "I'm sorry. I'm carrying on and making you uncomfortable."

"No, you're not. I was just wondering about my own family. That photo from my apartment shows only me and who I assume are my parents." She dug through her memories, trying to pull out one image from her childhood. She sighed as nothing came. Her childhood was behind a blank wall she couldn't penetrate. "I don't remember them at all. I don't remember losing them or how I reacted or even how they died. It's an odd feeling not remembering my own reaction to their deaths." She put her hands over her head, willing the memories to return. "Why can't I remember?"

He put his arm around her. "My memories aren't great, but at least I have them. I'm sorry. I can't imagine what you must be going through. I'm sorry for spilling my guts to you too. You have a lot more going on than a few bad family memories."

He took her hand and led them back toward the house.

"I like being here," she told him. "It's quiet and peaceful without feeling isolated. Whenever I think back to that tiny apartment, I wonder how I ever survived there. It all just seems so isolating. I can't imagine how lonely I must have been."

"It is beautiful here. I forgot how amazing this place could be. I suppose I let my own anger and bitterness color how I saw it." He pushed a hand through his hair. "I'm beginning to realize how I let my memories color everything about my life. I've just been floating along, not really making any decisions, allowing the decisions to make themselves."

"I doubt that's true. You made the decision to join the marines. You made the decision to open your business."

"Wilson really pushed me into that. I'm thankful he did, but it was all his idea."

"Well, he wanted you with him for a reason. Whitney must have trusted you too."

"I guess she did. She came to us because we were in the marines with her fiancé, Tony. He was killed in action in an explosion. Wilson and I brought his body back home to his family. They were all devastated and so were we. Tony was a good guy. One of the best. Whitney said she trusted us with her life because Tony had trusted us with his." He shook his head. "Look what that got her."

He shouldered a lot of guilt when it came to Whitney's death, but Jaycee knew better than anyone that he wasn't the one at fault. "You can't keep blaming yourself for what someone else did."

He stopped walking and looked at her. "Neither can

you. I see how much you blame yourself for breaking into that alarm. You feel responsible for her death, just as I do, when the truth is that we both need to stop shouldering the blame and place it where it belongs—with the man who killed her."

He was right…but it wasn't easy. Her face warmed as she thought about how she'd allowed herself to be fooled. If only she could remember if she'd done her due diligence, then forgiving herself wouldn't be so difficult. Had she really done everything she could to check out that man? Or had she reacted to his charm and Harry Jackson's recommendation?

She still couldn't see his face but she imagined him as a slick, car salesman type who thought he could sell anything to anyone. And he'd sold her a tale believable enough to pull her into a homicide.

"I'm sure you are good at your job, Jaycee, but you're also only human. This man, whoever he really is, was able to trick you. That's not your fault. There's evil in the world. People scheming and searching for a way to get what they want no matter who they hurt doing so."

She shuddered and he put his arm around her shoulders. She leaned into his embrace. It was nice. She sighed. "Why does the world have to be this way? Everything seems so difficult right now."

"I know, but it'll get better. We have to have faith that God will work everything out."

Jaycee stopped, surprised by his talk about God. She didn't remember much about her faith as it related to her life, but she felt like she'd made too many mistakes to earn anyone's forgiveness, especially God's.

He must have sensed her hesitation because he forced her to look at him. "Jaycee, this isn't your fault. None of this is your fault. You were tricked. Someone went to a lot of planning in order to fool you."

"But I'm the one who fell for it. I'm the dupe who believed."

"It's not your fault someone deceived you. You did your job. You weren't looking to hurt anyone."

"How do I know I didn't trust my gut? How do I know I didn't have reservations that I pushed aside or red flags that I missed?"

He pulled her to him and hugged her tightly. "I don't have those answers. But they don't really matter, Jaycee. Even if you knew the truth, you couldn't change it. It wouldn't change the fact that someone fooled you. You're not responsible for what some maniac did."

She pushed away a tear that threatened to release the dam. "I just wish I knew."

"Would it make a difference?"

She stared at him then shook her head. "I guess not."

"You and I are not responsible." He leaned back and sighed as if he'd just realized that for himself. "I know I took my eye off the ball. I know I relied on myself more than God. I may have some culpability that I'll have to live with, but I didn't kill Whitney. I didn't shoot her. Someone else did that, and he'll have to be the one to pay for it.

"Wilson quoted me a Bible verse after Whitney died. Romans 8 verse 1. 'There is therefore no condemnation to them who are in Christ Jesus.' I've done my best to stand on it. To claim it. But it's hard when I know I do hold some culpability. If I'd done something different, if I hadn't gotten wrapped up in the worldliness of fame, and blinded by my own press as security to the stars, I might have been more vigilant. I allowed vanity and pride to blind me to what I needed to do and Whitney died because of it. That's on me. I have to live with that and, maybe, you have stuff you'll have to live with too. It doesn't make us guilty, Jaycee. It doesn't make us responsible for what happened to her. That responsibility lies with the person who orchestrated all of this and the one who took her life."

His words made sense and she wanted to believe in them. She didn't think she was the kind of person who would do something like hacking into a person's security system for money and knowing it would lead to this. But she didn't really know herself, either, did she? She didn't know what kind of a person she really was.

Jaycee hoped he was right about her. She hoped she hadn't missed something.

However, at the end of the day, Brett was also right when he'd said it wouldn't make a difference. Whitney was still dead and the killer was still after Jaycee.

But, if she'd been in on the conspiracy, would the killer still need to silence her?

That thought gave her some peace.

She was being targeted because of what she knew.

He put his arm around her again as they walked back to the house. They hadn't made any progress in figuring out who was behind all of this, but she felt she knew Brett Harmon a little better. And maybe she knew herself better too.

She didn't deserve Brett's help, much less his attention toward her, but she sure wanted it.

And she couldn't deny she enjoyed the weight of his arm across her shoulders as they walked and the sound of deep laughter as he recounted shenanigans from his childhood here on the ranch.

Though one question was never far from her mind. Would he ever be able to truly forgive her for her part in Whitney's death?

# SEVEN

It felt like years since she'd been at her computer but it had only been a day. Jaycee awoke the next morning after sleeping more soundly and safely than she had in a while and decided she was ready to dive back into trying to figure out who was behind the attacks on her.

She found the den empty so she curled up on the couch and opened her laptop, thankful that Brett had remembered to retrieve it. She still had a lot of work to do to find out who was behind these attacks on her.

She glanced through the last name she'd been researching. Jack Milton. Oh yeah, the sleazy producer Whitney had included on her list of people who might have a grudge against her.

Too bad she hadn't told anyone what that grudge was.

Still, Jaycee could guess. From her internet search, she found blog posts and newspaper articles that mentioned a scandal involving a producer handing out prime roles for actresses who slept with him. Another accused him of assaulting several women. Whitney was listed on a social media post as one of those alleged victims.

She pulled up the post and clicked on the name of the woman who'd made it. Samantha Mason. One of the women who'd accused Milton of assault. Only, Jaycee couldn't find anywhere that Whitney had actually made an accusation against him, at least not online.

She sighed, unsure if this meant anything or not.

She stared at an image of Jack Milton. Was this the man who'd hired her to sabotage Whitney's security so he could kill her just to keep her from accusing him of assault? It seemed like a stretch. After all, multiple women had already accused him and he hadn't murdered any of them.

She closed her eyes and once again trying to picture the man who'd hired her. She saw herself sitting across from him at a café. She remembered laughing at something witty he'd said. But his face was still a blank to her.

She opened her eyes then quickly opened another browser and pulled up her own bank statements for the past few months. The visit to First United Bank had sparked a memory of the name of her bank and she'd quickly hacked in and found her accounts. At first glance, nothing had seemed suspicious. She'd been paid by wire transfer for her job of hacking into Brett's alarm system, but she hadn't been able to identify where the money had come from. It had been transferred from a shell company that was now closed. But if she could pinpoint the café where she'd met the man who'd hired her through a credit card charge, she might be able to access the café's security videos and get a better image of him. Or, even better, a credit card transaction with his name. It might be a false name but at least it would be something.

She scoured through her accounts but found no charges to anything that could have been a meetup with the man who'd hired her.

"You look like you're concentrating on something really hard."

Jaycee turned to see Abby had walked into the room.

"I guess I was. Ever since I realized this man had tricked me into becoming an accomplice for murder, I've been wracking my brain trying to remember him. The memory is so close, I can almost reach out and grab it. Only, I can't."

Abby touched her arm. "My mother always used to say that if you're wearing yourself out trying to think of something, the best thing you can do is try to forget it."

"But I've already forgotten it. That's the problem."

"No, she meant take your mind off of it. Give your brain a rest, Jaycee. Concentrate on something else for a while. Maybe that image you're struggling so hard to remember will come back to you."

"This man has already killed one woman and has tried to kill me, too, several times. What else am I going to concentrate on?"

"You've got a whole ranch to occupy your mind. Brett brought you here to keep you safe, but that doesn't mean you can't enjoy yourself too. We are taking advantage of the beautiful sunshine and the kids being out of school by going horseback riding. Why don't you come along with us? It'll be good for you to get out in the fresh air. I gather you haven't had a lot of that since this all started."

The thought of spending some time outside sounded nice. It looked like a pretty day. But she had to remember she hadn't come to Harmon Ranch to enjoy ranch life. "I don't think it's a good idea."

"You'll be perfectly safe. I'll even ask Luke to come along, if that would make you feel better. We'll lasso Brett, too, and make it an afternoon." Abby's face lit up. "I've got some boots you can borrow plus a hat for you to wear. Be right back." She hurried out before Jaycee could even object.

She was glad for the distraction and for the way Abby had accepted her here. She'd been worried about how the other woman would feel having her around the kids, knowing that someone was after her. Abby seemed unflappable. Jaycee admired that about her.

Abby returned with a pair of jeans, boots and a cowboy hat for Jaycee to change into. "I'm fixing a picnic lunch then we'll head out. Meet us in the kitchen whenever you're ready."

Jaycee closed her laptop then hurried upstairs to her room. Maybe Abby was right. She quickly changed into the clothes Abby had given her then went downstairs. Abby was in the kitchen with the kids, preparing sandwiches and bottled water.

Kenzie jumped to her feet when Jaycee entered. "Mama says you're going riding with us this afternoon."

Jaycee laughed at her enthusiasm. It was contagious.

Brett entered the kitchen, followed by Luke. He'd obviously overheard Kenzie's statement. "You're going riding?"

She shrugged. "I thought it might be nice to get outside for a while. Unless you don't think it's safe."

"No, it's safe. I didn't know you liked riding horses."

She suddenly realized she had no idea if she liked horses or not, or if she even knew how to ride. "I don't know either. I guess I'll find out."

"I'm going, too," Luke told him. "Why don't you come?"

Brett nodded. "I think I will come with you." He glanced at Jaycee and she smiled, liking that idea.

Abby finished loading up a cooler bag and some lunch bags. "Are we ready to head down to the stables?"

"Yes!" Kenzie and Dustin both jumped from their chairs and ran toward the door. Abby laughed as she and Luke followed behind them. "They don't have a lot of patience. We'll meet you there," she told Brett and Jaycee.

They left the house, trailing Luke, Abby and the kids.

Jaycee suddenly felt the need to explain her sudden desire to go riding with the group. "I've been wracking my brain trying to figure out who this guy is that hired me. It's driving me crazy. Abby saw me struggling and suggested I do something fun to take my mind off of it. She thought it might help me regain my memories if I stopped trying so hard."

He listened then nodded. "That's not bad advice. It might help. It surely can't hurt."

"I feel like I should be working on trying to figure this out though. I've been making my way down Whitney's list and I came across this movie producer. There have been several actresses who've accused him of assaulting them. I thought Whitney might be one of them and maybe he killed her to shut her up, but I haven't found any direct evidence that she made any accusations against him."

"Who is this producer?"

"His name is Jack Milton."

"I've met Jack. He was the head of the studio Whitney's show was on. She went to see him several times while I was protecting her. Surely, if something had been going on, she would have alerted me to it."

"Maybe. Maybe not. She did include him on her grudge list though. There has to be a reason for that."

He nodded. "If he's on the list then I'm sure someone from my team checked him out when we were first hired. I don't recall seeing anything that would concern me, but someone like that would have the money to pull off hiring you and setting up Albertson to take the fall. It's doubtful a producer would do his own dirty work, though, and risk being identified. He'd probably hire a middle man for the face-to-face work. You couldn't identify him as the man who hired you though?"

She shook her head. "Nope, that's still a blank. I'll start digging into Milton when we get back to the house."

They reached the barn and found Luke and his family already saddled up and ready to go. An older man with white hair reached out to shake Brett's hand.

"Brett, it's good to see you again. I heard you were coming back to the ranch."

"Hi, Ed. Yes, I'm back for a little while. This is Jaycee. We thought we would join Luke and them for a ride."

Ed nodded. "You've got some good riding options. Any of the starlings are in good shape and easy to handle."

Dustin's horse whinnied near her, causing Jaycee to startle and quickly move away. Brett grabbed her. "Don't spook him."

"I didn't mean to," she said. "I'm just rethinking this riding thing. I don't think I'm a horse person."

He chuckled. "Obviously not. Those muscles would be instinctive." He glanced at Luke. "We'll catch up with you."

As the family trotted away, Jaycee had the sudden urge to run back to the house and hide out in her bedroom. Brett took her arm. "It's okay. We'll ride together."

Ed grabbed a bridle and placed it on a horse in one of the stables. He walked it out and picked up some brushes. Brett stepped in. "I can help saddle him." He helped Ed brush the horse down then hurried to grab a saddle pad, the saddle and then the tack.

He walked the horse outside and climbed into the saddle. When he reached his hand down for Jaycee, she instinctively backed away. He chuckled and kept his hand out. "Do you trust me, Jaycee?"

She stared up into his green eyes and found herself lost in his gaze. She did trust him, and that frightened her more than the horse. Finally, she reached for his hand as Ed pulled up a set of steps and she climbed onto the back of the horse. Her heart jumped as she wrapped her arms around Brett's waist and held on. She couldn't tell if it was from fear or excitement.

He laughed and prodded the horse forward. "Everything's going to be okay. Try to relax."

She held on tightly as he guided the horse through a pasture and into an open field.

After a while, Jaycee relaxed and enjoyed the wind in her hair, the movement of the horse and the feel of Brett's muscles under her hands. He pulled the horse to a stop and she found herself smiling at the exhilaration of it all.

She leaned her head into Brett's back. "That was fun."

He laughed a deep, pleasing laugh that tickled her. "It was. It's been a while since I've ridden like that. I hope I didn't frighten you."

The giggling of the kids across the way echoed in her ears, but they were distant enough that she felt like she and Brett were in their own world. "You didn't." She felt more alive at the moment than she could remember since this nightmare had started. She felt…normal.

"Let's take a break and give the horse a chance to cool off." He helped lower her to the ground then climbed off. He tied the horse's reins to a nearby tree then settled on the ground a few feet away. Jaycee sat beside him on the grass, enjoying how carefree and relaxed he seemed right now. She'd never seen him so relaxed before. And so ruggedly handsome.

"How long has it been since you've gone horseback riding?"

"Years."

"It's good to see you laugh and relax."

He smiled and stroked her cheek. "You too."

He turned to her and all the air between them seemed

to evaporate. He wanted to kiss her. And she wanted him to.

He stroked her cheek and leaned in, but pulled back at the last moment. His breathing hitched and he dragged a hand through his hair.

He started to stand. "I'm sorry. I shouldn't have—"

"I didn't mind," she told him, surprising herself at her forwardness as she grabbed his arm and pulled him back to the ground.

He stared at her then picked at a blade of grass. "I'm attracted to you, Jaycee. I don't deny that. You're beautiful and kind and strong. But after what happened to Whitney—" he tossed the blade of grass away "—I can't allow myself to get distracted, not when your life is in danger."

It seemed her involvement in Whitney's death would always come between them.

He gave a loud sigh and stood. "Maybe we should head back to the house."

She glanced over at Luke and Abby sitting on a blanket across the field, heads down in intimate conversation as their kids played nearby, and her heart ached for something like that. She hadn't even realized she'd wanted it until just now.

But she could never have that until she recovered her memories and discovered who wanted her dead.

Brett may never forgive her for her role in Whitney's death, and she couldn't really blame him, but she instinctively knew she was ready to stop being alone. She was ready to live her life again.

That meant getting back to work. She crawled to her

feet too. "That's a good idea. I should get back to digging through Jack Milton's scandal-ridden life. There might be something there."

He reached for her hand to help her.

Shots rang out, sending them both tumbling to the ground. The horse bucked and snorted, startled by the noise, and the kids screamed.

Her heart raced as Brett's weight covered her.

Another shot rang out.

Brett grabbed her arms. "Run!" He pushed her toward some brush behind the tree where he'd tied the horse and she ran for cover while ducking to be a smaller target.

The killer had found her again.

Brett ran behind Jaycee as another shot fired. It whizzed past him. Too close.

He jumped into a row of brush for cover then pushed her flat to the ground. "Stay low," he commanded.

He scanned the horizon and spotted a glint from the scope. Given the distance, it could only be one thing—sniper rifle.

He scanned the field and eyed his cousin taking cover with his family. Luke held up his cell phone and a moment later, Brett's rang.

"Is anyone hurt?" was Brett's first question. He would hate it if Abby or the kids had been hit because someone was after him and Jaycee.

"They're fine," Luke told him. "Scared, but no injuries. Any idea who's shooting at us?"

"I've got a sniper at ten o'clock," Brett said.

Luke agreed. "I see him. I'll phone Caleb to come

check it out. You and Jaycee should get out of here. I've got my rifle. I'll cover your escape."

His rifle didn't have the range to reach the sniper and they both knew it, but Brett understood Luke's meaning. The sniper was after him and Jaycee, not Luke and his family.

"I'll be right back," he told Jaycee.

She grabbed his arm, panic filling her face. "Where are you going?"

"I'm going to get our horse and we're getting out of here. We can't stay pinned down." The horse was a bigger target for the sniper to hit, but they could get out of range faster on it than on foot. He had to risk it.

He climbed to his feet and headed toward the tree where he'd tied the horse, shielding his movement with the horse's body as best he could until he reached it. Once he did, he quickly untied him, climbed into the saddle and headed for Jaycee.

Gunfire erupted from the sniper but Brett moved quickly as Luke returned fire.

He urged the horse into the brush where Jaycee hid, then lifted her up behind him.

Just as she settled, shots fired again. The horse started and she nearly slid as he bucked. Brett held on to the reins as Jaycee clung to his jacket.

"Get out of here!" she cried.

Brett wasted no time.

He spun the horse around and took off. He felt her tremble but couldn't stop to comfort her until they were out of range.

Their safe, protective hideout had been breached.

# EIGHT

Brett kicked the horse, urging him faster through the field. He didn't stop or slow down. He didn't want to make the horse stumble but whoever was shooting at them wasn't giving up. They had to get out of range before his bullet found its mark.

His mind raced with thoughts about how he'd let his guard down but he tried not to dwell on them. Getting Jaycee to safety had to be his primary concern.

He spotted the old hay barn and relief flooded him. They could take cover there and probably were already out of the range of the sniper. He directed the horse behind the barn then slid off and helped Jaycee down. She was trembling with fear, but they would be safe inside.

He stayed close to the building as they sneaked into the front entrance. He closed the barn door behind them and sighed in relief. The sniper wouldn't be able to reach them in here.

He took out his phone and dialed Luke. "What's your status?"

"I think we're okay," he said, causing Brett to let out

another relieved breath. "He stopped firing once you and Jaycee were away."

It made him cringe to think of leaving Luke and his family that way, but they'd been the target, not Abby and the kids.

"Where are you?" Luke asked him.

"We've taken cover in the old hay barn. Call Caleb and have him bring a car. I need to get Jaycee to safety as quickly as possible, then I want to find this sniper."

Luke agreed and ended the call.

He turned to Jaycee and pulled her to him, wrapping his arms around her. She was trying to hold it together, but she'd been through so much. She had to be nearing her breaking point.

"We're okay," he assured her. "My cousins are coming. We're going to find this shooter. Everything will be okay."

Yet, even as he reassured her, he wasn't so certain.

If their location had been compromised, very few people would have known where they'd gone. And only a few people in his office would have the ability to shoot at them from this distance.

He was looking for one of his own, a former sniper. Even more confirmation of his suspicions.

They had several former snipers on their staff…but only one of them knew his and Jaycee's whereabouts.

*Wilson.*

The roar of an engine pulled him away from Jaycee. He drew his gun, just in case, then peeked through the door and spotted a car heading their way across the field. Caleb was behind the wheel and Brett spotted Luke, Abby and the kids already inside.

He holstered his weapon. "It's Caleb."

Caleb pulled up to the doors and Brett ushered Jaycee into the vehicle before climbing in behind her.

"You two okay?" Caleb asked.

"We're fine." He glanced at Abby and the kids. "Everyone okay?"

Abby nodded as she hugged Dustin to her. "Yes."

"I'm so sorry this happened," Jaycee said, but Abby shushed her.

"This wasn't your fault."

Abby was right. It was his fault for not being more careful. But Jaycee should have been safe here. No one was supposed to know where they were.

They made it to the house and Luke ushered his family inside. Brett would phone Ed to send someone to get the horse but, for now, he wanted Jaycee inside the safety of the farmhouse.

"Stay inside and keep away from the windows," Brett instructed her as he closed the blinds and curtains. The sniper couldn't shoot what he couldn't see and since they had no idea where he was or if he would even return, they had to take precautions. "We'll be back as soon as we can."

Jaycee grabbed his sleeve. "You're not going back out there, are you?" The panic in her face was clear but he had no choice if he wanted to find out who was behind this attack.

He touched her hand. "I'm sure the sniper is gone by now, but we need to make sure and look for evidence. I can't risk him targeting you every time you step out of the door. Don't worry. We'll be fine."

Caleb stood at the door. "I'll stay here with them and guard the place. I can start taking statements about what happened too."

Brett thanked him for remaining. He felt better knowing someone was watching out for Jaycee.

"I'll also call Ed and have him send someone to look for the horses."

Brett and Luke loaded onto ATVs and headed out. They'd both seen the glare from the scope and had a good idea of where the sniper might have been.

They headed up to the hill and finally found a sniper's nest, but it didn't give up much evidence. The marksman was long gone and he'd cleaned up after himself well.

Luke noticed that too. "He's good. Probably a professional."

That was what Brett was afraid of. B&W had several former military snipers on their team…including Wilson.

Luke glanced around then motioned to his cousin. "Tire tracks."

Luke nodded. "I'll get a plaster kit and come back and make molds of them. They might give us a clue who we're dealing with. I'll also have Caleb see about accessing security video. Maybe he passed by the gates and we'll see someone from out of town you recognize."

Brett hoped he wouldn't, but it was more and more likely he would. He was convinced more than ever that whomever was after Jaycee was working with someone in his office or, worse, *was* someone in his office.

They headed back to the farmhouse.

He found Jaycee huddled beside Abby on the couch,

her hands twisted with worry. She looked ready to flee at any moment and he pushed aside an urge to go to her and hug her until she calmed down. She had a reason to be frightened. The danger wasn't over.

When she spotted him, she jumped to her feet and ran into his arms, pressing her face into his chest. He put his arms around her. "Hey, I told you I would be back."

"I know. I was just so scared."

Caleb stood. "Did you two find anything?"

"Not much," Brett said.

Luke agreed. "We found some tire tracks. I'm going to get my kit and go back and take a mold. Maybe we can match them to a car or truck in the area at the time of the shooting through video surveillance."

Caleb nodded. "I'll call Hansen and have him start pulling video footage coming in and out of town. Of course, the sniper could have gone the other way, bypassing town completely. There are no cameras headed toward the highway."

Brett sighed. "I know and you're probably right but—"

His cousin held up his hand. "We'll still check it out. I've already taken Jaycee's statement about what happened. Let me get yours too."

He didn't want to leave Jaycee but he needed to. "I'll just be in the kitchen, okay?" She nodded then released him.

He walked into the kitchen and gave Caleb a play-by-play.

Caleb sighed and closed his notebook. "Who knew you and Jaycee were coming here, Brett?"

He glanced at his cousin. "Only a few people in my office even know about this place."

"Well, you said you thought it had to be someone inside your office who spiked Jaycee's drink. It looks like you were right after all."

He pulled his hand through his hair. "I can't believe this. Someone in my office just tried to kill us and they tried to kill Jaycee. He might have even been involved in Whitney's murder."

"I wouldn't recommend leaving the house until we know more. I'll double patrols in town and try to locate anyone suspicious or unfamiliar in the area." Caleb stopped and placed his hand on Brett's shoulder. "You're not alone in this, cuz. Luke and I are here for you. We've got your back. We'll make sure nothing happens to you or Jaycee while you're here."

He appreciated his cousin's words. His statement did make Brett feel better. He was used to working with a team. He and Wilson had been each other's anchors since they'd met in the marines. He'd always been able to count on his friend.

He tried to tell himself he still could, but he just wasn't sure anymore.

He decided not to trust anyone, including his business partner, until he knew more. Except for Luke and Caleb, he and Jaycee were on their own.

He stared into the living room at Jaycee and resisted the urge again to go to her. He'd gotten too attached to her and today proved that. He couldn't believe he'd tried to kiss her before everything had gone sideways. He felt his face warm at the thought of how much he'd wanted to kiss her. He had no business even thinking of her that way. They were on the hunt for a killer and her life was at risk. He'd let down his guard with Whitney and look what had happened.

He couldn't allow history to repeat itself.

Luke came up beside him. "She's pretty amazing, isn't she?"

"Yes, she is," Brett agreed.

"I can tell you're wild about her."

He looked at his cousin. "It doesn't matter what I think about her. I have to keep my head clear and my attention focused on keeping her safe."

"It's okay to admit that you're attracted to her. You are human, after all."

Brett rubbed the back of his neck. He knew his cousin meant well. "You wouldn't understand. It's complicated."

"Try me."

Brett slid into a chair at the kitchen table. Okay, if his cousin really wanted to know, he would tell him.

"How about the fact that she took down my security system. She hacked my system and, because of that, a woman was murdered. How can I forget that?"

Luke slid into the opposite chair. "You can't, but you can also acknowledge that it wasn't her fault. It's not her you can't forgive, is it? The person you're really having trouble forgiving is yourself. If you did your best to keep her safe then you should have nothing to feel guilty about."

That was the rub, though, wasn't it? He couldn't stop wondering if he had indeed done his best. Had he been too arrogant about his own skills? Too focused on the write-ups about him in the news columns? He pulled a hand through his hair and sighed. He didn't know.

"I know a thing or two about learning to forgive someone," Luke stated. He got up and glanced into the living room at his own wife and kids. "When I first learned that Kenzie was my daughter and that Abby had kept that from me, I was so angry at her. I thought I would never be able to forgive her for that."

"Yet, you did," Brett said. "How?"

"It wasn't easy to put those feelings aside, but I found that being with her was more important to me than being righteous. She made a mistake, and we all paid the price for it, but anger and resentment weren't going to change the facts. In the end, I just wanted her more than I wanted to be angry about the situation."

"That simple, huh?"

Luke chuckled. "No, not that simple. But doable." He turned to face Brett. "Anyone can see that you're falling for Jaycee. There's still a lot you don't know about her, but I'm just saying don't let your anger and fear be the thing that keeps you from being happy. I've seen it happen far too often." He glanced at the picture on the wall of their grandfather, Chet Harmon. "Case in point. I'm not sure he lived one happy day after losing his sons."

"I understand how difficult that had to be."

"Yes, it was. I'm not saying it wasn't hard, but he could never move past it. He pushed everyone away after that. He kept us all at arm's length so he wouldn't get hurt again. And what did it get him? He died alone with no family."

"Caleb was here."

"Have you spoken to Caleb recently? He'll tell you he was living here but there was never any closeness between them. Grandpa sealed off his heart, shielded himself from pain. Don't be like him, Brett."

He took in Luke's words. He'd wondered how his cousin could recover enough from discovering he had a teenage daughter to marrying the woman who'd lied to him. How could he hold no ill will toward her for stealing all those years away?

He thought about his stepdad and all he'd lost. He'd lost his first wife and daughter in a car accident then his wife—Brett's mother. Grief and pain seemed to follow him yet he never let it get to him. He kept on, enjoying life, and had even started dating again.

He stared back at Jaycee and felt his heart skip a beat. He couldn't deny the attraction to her but he wasn't sure he could ever get past the role she'd played in all of this. Yes, he believed she'd been tricked. Yes, he believed she was merely a pawn in someone's master game. Yes, she was doing everything she could to try to make amends and her life was at risk for doing so. Yet, her involvement cut him.

Was Luke right? Was he taking out his own guilt and frustration on the wrong person?

Was it really himself he needed to forgive?

Jaycee did her best to push aside her fear and angst. She had to focus on getting through this and figuring out who was after her. The closed curtains reminded her that her life was not her own. She was being targeted, and no one could forget that.

She pulled up her laptop. She'd told Brett that she would dig more into Jack Milton to figure out if he could be involved in Whitney's murder. She used keywords to search the internet for Whitney Warren and pulled up more than she could slog through about her murder, including several links that appeared to blame her security detail, aka Brett, for her death. She quickly moved past them and changed her keywords, adding Milton's name to the mix.

Several posts popped up on social media sites, including the one blog post she'd seen earlier that named names of actresses who had been victimized by Milton. She glanced at the name of the person who'd written the blog—Samantha Mason, another actress who'd made multiple claims against Milton and was trying to bring him to justice.

Jaycee had to wonder if Whitney had shared with her that she'd been a victim of Milton's or if the actress had included her name without verification. Jaycee quickly found her online and sent her a message, asking if they could speak about Whitney and the accusations.

She moved on to the next name on Whitney's list and made it through all the remaining names without finding anything out of the ordinary.

And still she hadn't heard back from Samantha Mason.

Unless the actress would speak to her and could confirm Whitney had been planning to publicly accuse Milton of assault, Jaycee would have to mark him off the list.

Brett entered, carrying his own laptop. "I've been

going through the company's personnel files. I've flagged two. The first is Sean Knight, our part-time consultant who sets up the alarm systems. I haven't been able to verify some of his information."

"He set up those security alarms. Why would he need to hire me to do something he could have done himself with very little oversight?"

He sighed. "You make a good point. Still." He clicked on a photograph of Sean. "Does he look familiar?"

She studied his face but nothing came to her. "No, nothing. What's so suspicious about him?"

"I contacted the organization he said he was joining for his missionary trip and they didn't even have an overseas trip scheduled."

"Maybe he joined in with another organization."

"It's possible but every time I've talked to him, he's gone on and on about this organization."

It still didn't make sense to her why another expert would need to trick her into hacking their systems, but if Brett was suspicious of him then so was she.

"Okay, suspicious personnel file number two." He clicked on a link then spun the laptop back around for her to see. "Mitch Dearborn. Our last hire six months ago. His employment history seems to have holes in it. I phoned his last two employers and neither of them had ever heard of him."

"That does seem odd."

His face darkened. "Wilson had to have verified his employment when he hired him. He had to have known."

"Do you think Wilson is hiding something?" She hated to think that his best friend and business partner would betray him that way, but they had to look at all scenarios.

"I don't want to think it, Jaycee, but I need to know for certain. Is there any way to get a look into their bank accounts? If someone is paying one of my employees to go after you, I need to know who."

She nodded. "If their paychecks are direct deposited, I can follow that link to view their accounts." She saw the conflict on his face. "Are you sure you want to do this?"

His face hardened. He needed to know the truth. They both did. "Do it," he told her.

He gave her the code to access the personnel records for the company. She pulled up Mitch Dearborn's file, found his direct deposit information then used that to access his bank account.

"What did you find?" he asked, glancing over her shoulder.

"Nothing," she noted. "The only money coming into his account is from B&W. He pays his bills and buys takeout a little too often, but everything looks normal."

"He could have another account he uses."

"He could, but I don't have a way to access that account without knowing what it is."

Brett stood and rubbed his face. "You're right. What about Sean's?"

She took the same route to access Sean's bank account, but she found no large deposits there either. "I do see a charge for a plane ticket but no transactions in the past few days. It's possible he's using cash on his trip."

"Maybe."

"Is it possible we're thinking about this all wrong? Maybe it's not someone outside paying one of your people, but one of your people who is behind all of this."

He pondered that for a moment. "Why would anyone in my office want to hurt Whitney?"

"I don't know." She wished one of the leads she'd been pursuing on Whitney's grudge list had panned out. She checked her messages again and found a response from Samantha Mason. Excited, she called Brett over as she read it. "She's willing to meet with us and discuss Whitney's relationship with Jack Milton."

He slid into the spot beside her. "Ask if she would be willing to video chat with us."

Jaycee relayed the message and, to her surprise, Samantha Mason replied right away. "She's fine with it. She sent us a link to chat."

Brett nodded and Jaycee clicked on the link Samantha had provided. A video screen popped up and, moments later, they connected.

Samantha Mason greeted them both warmly. "I'm glad you contacted me," she said. "I was heartbroken when I heard about Whitney's murder. In this business, we depend on our fans, but when one of them turns violent, it's a horrific thing."

Brett leaned forward. "We don't believe it was a fan that killed Whitney."

Her eyes widened. "But the news claims the police have a man in custody. Someone that confessed to killing her."

"There are extenuating circumstances that the police are overlooking," Brett told her. "Someone hired

Jaycee here to hack into our security systems. That allowed the killer to get to Whitney. We think whoever hired her also set up this fan to take the fall for Whitney's murder."

Her eyes widened. "Oh my. Who hired you?" she asked Jaycee.

"That's the problem. I can't remember. I was attacked and some of my memories are missing. However, we're looking into one of Whitney's producers, Jack Milton."

Understanding dawned on her. "You think Jack is responsible for her death?"

"We're only looking into him for now," Brett reiterated. "But we found a site where you claimed he had assaulted Whitney and that she was planning to file charges against him. Was there any truth to that account?"

"She confided to me that Jack offered her a role in his next big movie. She was excited about it, but when he told her the cost of getting the role, she tried to leave his office. He tried to force himself on her but she managed to get away. I urged her to join my petition, but she wasn't sure she was ready to do so. We could have brought this man to justice together."

"How many people are on this list?" Jaycee asked. "I noticed multiple names on your post. Is there any reason why he would target Whitney specifically?"

"She was credible. That's why I wanted her to go to the police. She didn't have any skeletons in her closet yet, like the rest of us had. She hadn't yet compromised herself. Ultimately, she was believable. I know she was struggling with what to do. I invited her to come to Dallas. I hoped I could convince her to join me in this crusade, but she was hesitant. At least, until that phone call."

"What phone call?"

"The last time we spoke, Whitney told me Jack had called her and tried to talk her out of making any accusations against him. She said he threatened her."

"Why wouldn't she have mentioned this to me?"

Samantha sighed. "You were friends with her fiancé, correct? She was afraid of disappointing his memory. Plus, she knew she had a stalker and she thought she was in more danger from him than Jack. I tried to warn her to tell you and the police. She didn't know Jack the way I do. I've seen his violent side before so I took the threat seriously. I don't think Whitney did."

So, they had a movie producer with a history of violent behavior who'd tried to assault Whitney then threatened her if she came forward. Jaycee wondered if Detective Hennessy knew about him and, if he did, if it would change his opinion of the man he had in custody. It seemed to Jaycee that Lincoln Albertson was likely more a fall guy than an actual perpetrator. What were the chances that Whitney had been killed by a single, unstable stalker when someone had hired Jaycee? She might be able to prove Albertson's innocence, too, if she could only get her hands on his plane ticket and discover who paid for it.

They thanked Samantha for her information then ended the video chat.

Jaycee turned to Brett. "What are we going to do about Milton?" It seemed likely that he was the man who'd hired her, or at least, the one who'd paid her for the job. He had to be behind this. He was the only one they'd found so far who had the money, the connections, and, according to Samantha, had a reputation that Whitney threatened to ruin.

"Don't be so quick to jump to conclusions. We don't have anything to tie Milton to Whitney's death or to the attacks against you. We have to stick with what we can prove."

"Which isn't much."

He rubbed his chin and stood. "I'm not saying Milton isn't involved, but I keep going back to Wilson. He overlooked employment holes in Mitch's file. He knew we were here. Plus, he was a marine sniper. He has the skills to target us out in that field. As much as I don't want to go down that road, we have to. I can't believe he'd have a grudge against Whitney, so I'm still working on the assumption that someone, possibly Milton, is paying someone in our office to try to get to you. Start with his financials. If someone is paying him, it will show up."

She watched him walk out of the room. He was torn about this decision but he was right. They had to do it. If Wilson was their mole, they needed to know about it.

The effect this was having on Brett was clear. He was having a difficult time grasping that his best friend and business partner might be the one who'd betrayed him.

She took a deep breath then pulled up Wilson Jarrett's personnel file. *God, if You're out there, please don't let me find something that will cause Brett more pain.*

She turned her attention to Wilson, Brett's partner

and former marine squad brother. She back-traced his bank account to look for large deposits.

*Please don't be any. Please don't be any.*

A $50,000 payment had been deposited into his account the day after Whitney died.

Her heart fell. Was that the price for murdering someone these days?

Brett was going to be devastated.

She did her best to trace where the money had come from, but it ultimately led to an account that belonged to a private attorney. That was as far as she could trace it.

Maybe his laptop would provide the answers she needed. She could easily hack into it by accessing the company's Wi-Fi. She didn't want to alert him to what she was doing yet, so she first dialed his office and when he didn't answer his direct line, she dialed the switchboard and asked Trish his whereabouts.

"He's been out with a client all day," Trish explained. "You want me to have him call you when he returns?"

"No, thanks. I'll text him my question," Jaycee responded. She hated the subterfuge but it was necessary. She didn't want to remote dial into his computer only to have him sitting at it and watching everything she was doing. She could have also activated his webcam to make sure he wasn't there but, if he had been, it would have been too late to hide her activities.

She logged into his computer and turned on the webcam now, breathing a sigh of relief when no one looked back at her. She kept it as well as the microphone on so that if anyone entered the office, she would know.

Her first task was to perform a search of his hard

drive for files that might be suspicious. Most of the ones that popped up were related to the business and mundane stuff like payroll, employee benefits, insurance, clients and invoices.

She saw a file with Brett's name on it. She clicked on the icon and noticed multiple articles Wilson had downloaded and saved about Whitney's murder and Brett's—and their company's—names included. She didn't spend a lot of time on the file as it didn't strike her as odd. Of course, he was worried about his business. He would need to stay aware of the publicity surrounding the case and his business partner.

Only the next file she located—this one labeled "Whitney"—proved to be another story. She clicked the icon and was inundated with image after image of Whitney Warren. Photos from magazines and online images and, what looked to her, to be photographs taken of Whitney unaware, doing things like buying groceries or grabbing a coffee at a café. These looked like the images a paparazzo might take of someone or possibly even a private investigator trying to catch her in something noteworthy and payable. Of course, celebrities often hired photographers to follow them around and take pictures of them doing these kinds of things but Whitney looked completely unaware in most of these photos.

Whatever these images were for, they gave Jaycee chills. Whitney had confessed to Brett that she felt she was being watched all the time. These photographs seemed to indicate she had been.

Why did Wilson have them?

She copied Wilson's computer files to her drive to show Brett what she'd found. Was it possible Wilson had been obsessed with Whitney and he was behind this all along? That didn't account for the money in his account, but it was all adding up to seem like Wilson might be involved. She leaned back and shook her head, tears filling her eyes.

Brett was not going to be happy about this.

Low voices sounded from Wilson's computer microphone then she heard the door open. Someone was entering the office. She quickly ended her remote access and closed her laptop. Wilson Jarrett had just jumped to the top of the list of suspects.

He had the means and sophistication to hire her and his obsession with Whitney seemed apparent. Had he killed Whitney?

And when would he try coming after Jaycee again?

# NINE

Jaycee's discovery slammed hard into Brett. He scrolled through the multiple images of Whitney she'd found on Wilson's computer. They weren't just shots from magazine or news sites either. They were shots from a camera, either a paparazzo following her…or a stalker.

Was Wilson the mysterious Joe Cleveland? Or had he been hired by him to commit murder?

He rubbed a hand through his hair, his mind unable to comprehend this. He'd had his suspicions but he'd never really believed Wilson was involved…not until now. "How could I have missed this?" Had his best friend and partner been obsessed with Whitney?

He tried to think back to see if there were any signs he'd missed or overlooked. He couldn't think of any right off hand. Wilson had always been supportive of Brett protecting Whitney. He'd been the one to encourage him to take the assignment, claiming he had too much administrative paperwork to do to really give it his best. He hadn't checked in with them excessively.

But the more Brett thought about it, he hadn't been

overly upset over Whitney's death either. To be fair, he'd never been the sort of guy to get emotional. He saw a problem and tackled it without emotion. That was just the way he'd always been ever since Brett had known him, so he'd just assumed he was doing the same with the fiasco over Whitney's murder and the ding it had caused to their reputations and business.

He'd been working the problem…or so it seemed to Brett.

But what had he really been doing behind the scenes?

Brett shook his head and pushed the laptop away, standing and pacing. "I don't want to believe this. I can't think of one reason why he would be involved."

Jaycee pulled up another screen and turned the laptop around to show him. "I also found a large deposit in his bank account. Is it possible he was taking money to subvert her security or keep someone informed of her movements?"

Anger grabbed him and took hold. "This is Wilson. I've known him for ten years. I trusted him with my life in combat. I cannot believe for one moment that he could be involved in any of this. He isn't the kind of person to put someone's life at risk and he isn't the type of person to betray me."

She sighed and closed the laptop. "You may be right, but if it were anyone else, you would investigate it, wouldn't you? You can't let your feelings for your friend cloud your judgment."

Her words hit him like a ton of bricks. He'd already allowed his friendship with Whitney to cause him to let his guard down with disastrous results. She was dead…

and now Wilson might have been behind it. He shook his head again, his first instinct to disbelieve his own gut reaction, but Jaycee was right. He couldn't turn a blind eye to this evidence. He'd asked her to check everyone out. He couldn't fault her for finding something because of it.

"Okay. We'll go back to Dallas tomorrow and check out his office and see if we can find more evidence that ties him to this. I want to talk to him. I want to look him in the eye and see for myself that he's involved."

She nodded. "I think that's a good idea."

He picked up the photograph of the man at the bank captured on security cameras blackmailing the bank manager. If he squinted just right, it could be Wilson. He sighed, frustrated by the uncertainty and being pulled in different directions.

"We should show the bank manager a photo of Wilson and see if he can identify him. I assume you don't recognize him as the man who hired you?" She'd met Wilson and hadn't indicated she knew him, but that could be because of the amnesia.

"I don't," she said. "I'll email his picture to Harry Jackson. In fact, I'll email the others' pictures too to be thorough."

That was a good idea.

He'd already lost Whitney. He didn't want to lose another friend, but he wouldn't risk Jaycee's safety by not acting when he knew he should. "My security firm isn't sounding so secure. How did this happen?" He fell to the couch.

She scooted closer and sidled up to him. “It’s going to be okay. We’ll figure this out together.”

He reached out and stroked her cheek. He wasn’t sure what he would do without her by his side. All his doubts about her had long ago faded. Even with gaps in her memory, she knew what she was doing.

What he wouldn’t give to have all the facts. Apparently, he’d had his head stuck in the ground for far too long.

His mind was reeling. His entire life seemed to be falling around him and he had no way to stop it. Was this God’s way of clearing out his life for getting so caught up in the fame and news coverage about himself? He felt his face warm at how foolish he’d been. His pride had gotten Whitney killed and nearly taken down Jaycee. Now, it seemed it had sunk into his business as well.

They left the ranch early the next morning and the drive to Dallas gave him time to think about his reaction. He’d changed his mind about confronting Wilson. His mind still wouldn’t comprehend that his friend could be involved. He needed to see for himself what Wilson had been up to.

Brett pulled up his cell phone tracker. Wilson’s location data was turned off, so he couldn’t be tracked. Was that because he’d been in Jessup yesterday shooting at them? The thought burned him but he was doing his best not to jump to conclusions.

He drove by Wilson’s apartment. His car was missing from its spot, which indicated he wasn’t home. He tried the gym Wilson frequented next and spotted him walking out.

*Gotcha.*

Now he would see for himself what his so-called friend was up to when he wasn't in the office.

"Are you sure this is a good idea?" Jaycee asked him as they parked the car and waited outside a coffee shop.

Brett raised the camera he used for surveillance and zoomed in to get a better look at Wilson as he talked on his phone while pacing in front of the coffee shop. "It's fine. I just want to observe him for a while to see if I've missed something."

And it seemed he'd missed a lot while he'd been off guarding Whitney.

Wilson was acting stranger than usual today. He'd claimed he was spending his time dealing with clients but, for the past six hours, Brett and Jaycee had followed him from the gym to the bank, an attorney's office, to an electronics store and to a motorcycle dealership.

He seemed to be blowing through the $50k he'd received. Had his friend and partner sold out Whitney for a big payday? Was he obsessed with her? Or had those photos been merely part of a job for him?

And with their business fading from this scandal, how could Wilson justify making extravagant purchases?

Brett sighed. He'd seen enough to make him suspect his friend was involved in some way.

Brett's phone dinged with an email notification. He glanced at the screen and saw it was from his security guard friend at the hotel. It must be the internal video surveillance he'd promised to send over. He opened it up.

"My friend just sent me the video from the security feeds at the hotel the day of the murder. Let's go somewhere and look at it."

He wasn't sure he was ready to confront Wilson yet. If his friend was involved in something nefarious, a confrontation could get ugly. He wanted to have all the evidence in place first.

They drove to a coffee shop where Jaycee could connect to the Wi-Fi. He sent her the link to the video and she opened it on her laptop. The image of Albertson popped up on the screen.

"There he is," he said, pointing the man out to Jaycee. "We need to keep an eye on him and see what he does."

He stood outside the hotel building for hours. Brett noticed he checked his phone several times but mostly kept his eye on the hotel. He couldn't help but note he was looking high up. Whitney's hotel room had been on the eighth floor. Could he have known that? And, if he had, how? Brett had made those reservations himself and only a few people had known about her location. Wilson had been one of them.

About an hour before the murder, the time stamp on the video surveillance showed Albertson walk out of range of the cameras. He didn't return and none of the interior cameras caught sight of him. He'd either disguised himself well or he hadn't gone inside.

"Fast forward to after the murder."

She advanced the video but they didn't see him exit

the hotel any time after the murder and before the police arrived on scene.

She leaned back in her seat. "All this shows is that he was there."

Brett rubbed his chin. "It's compelling because it places him at the scene of the crime within an hour of it happening. That, along with his obsessive behaviors toward her would be enough to sway a jury."

She glanced at him. "Maybe Albertson did kill her. How else would he have been there at just the right time? His history shows he's from Florida. He followed her to Dallas. That looks very damaging to him."

"This still doesn't explain the man who paid you to hack our system or the money that Wilson was paid."

"Maybe Albertson was the dupe. They led him there to kill her. They might even have paid him to do it."

"No, the police would have found the money when they arrested him. I doubt he needed money though. Access to her might have been enough for him. If he was truly obsessed to the point of killing her, maybe someone led him there, hoping he would do the deed."

"That's not a great plan. How would they know he would go through with it? He might have backed out at the last minute or realized he was too much in love with her to kill her. He doesn't have a criminal record of violence. No one could have been certain he would go through with it."

Brett heaved a sigh. Jaycee was right. Setting this guy up to kill Whitney didn't make any sense. Albertson might have been her stalker, but whoever planned all of this wouldn't be able to depend on him to go through with the task. Either they'd caught a break… or Lincoln Albertson hadn't been the one to burst into her hotel room and kill her.

"I would still like to know how Albertson got to Dallas. Did he drive or fly? And, if he flew, did someone else pay for the ticket?"

"I've already thought of that. There's no way to find out without knowing which airline he took and on what date. I might be able to find out if I had that information."

A thought suddenly occurred to Brett. "If he flew, he probably has that information on his cell phone in an app or an email or even a text message from the airline. I'm sure the police confiscated it when he was arrested."

"Do you think Detective Hennessy would let us see it?"

Hennessy could be tough but Brett was sure he wanted to solve this case as much as they did. "It doesn't hurt to ask, does it?"

They walked back to the car and headed for the police station.

As usual, since he'd known him, Hennessy was in a foul mood. He grumbled when he saw Brett. "What do you want, Harmon?"

"I wanted to talk to you about Lincoln Albertson. Do you still have him in custody?"

"We do, but now he's recanting his earlier confession. He claims he never laid a finger on Whitney."

"Did he say why he confessed?"

Hennessy stopped and turned to him. "He doesn't have to. Why are you here, Harmon?"

"We were wondering about Albertson and how he got to town. Did he fly in or drive from Florida?"

"He flew. Arrived the same day of the murder. We have him on video standing outside her hotel for hours. I can place him at the scene and, with the escalating letters he sent her, we have enough to build a case. We've got our killer despite his recanted confession."

"Is there any way we can look at his cell phone?"

"Why?"

"We believe there's a bigger conspiracy going on here, Hennessy. Someone hired Jaycee to infiltrate our systems and compromise Whitney's security. I think whoever did that, also set up Albertson to take the fall for her murder. If so, whoever it was probably also paid for his plane ticket here. If we can look at his cell phone at the airline app or his email, we might be able to prove that and find out."

The detective seemed to think about that for a minute then nodded. "That's a good idea." He led them to an interview room and opened the door. "Wait here while I go down to the evidence room." He was gone for several minutes but returned with a box of items related to the case. He set it on the table and opened the box. He took out an evidence bag with the cell phone inside.

Brett's heart raced. This could be the moment that everything clicked and they finally figured out who was behind all of this. He was still hoping against hope that he was wrong about Wilson and the facts weren't what he thought they were.

Hennessy took out the cell phone and powered it up. He scrolled through until he found the airline's email with Albertson's flight information. "Here we go. He flew into the Dallas airport. It looks like his flight was paid for by—" He stopped and looked at Brett.

"What is it? Does it show who paid for the ticket?"

Hennessy turned the phone so he and Jaycee could see the screen for confirmation. "Albertson's flight into Dallas was paid for by a third party, but it only shows a partial credit card. However, this email was copied to B&W Security. Did your company pay to bring this man here?"

Brett glanced at the screen and saw the confirmation. The email had gone to the accounts payable email so that didn't help pinpoint who in the office had paid, but Brett recognized the last four digits of the card number as one that belonged to the company. His and Wilson's were only a few digits apart, and Brett certainly hadn't paid for this ticket.

He sat back in his seat as that information slammed into him. His business had paid to bring a stalker to Dallas. All the while the company had been hired to protect Whitney, someone at B&W had been plotting against her.

They'd brought Albertson out here to set him up to take the fall for Whitney's murder.

Even Hennessy seemed surprised by the revelation. "You want to tell me why your company paid for this man's ticket, Brett?"

"I think my partner, Wilson Jarrett, might be involved in all of this. I don't have the proof yet, but everything seems to point that way."

Hennessy put the phone away then boxed it and sat

down. He glanced at Jaycee. "I take it you haven't gotten your memory back and still can't identify the person who hired you?"

She shook her head. Brett could tell that was still eating at her. He, too, wished she could remember. That would have made all of this a lot simpler.

But would he have even trusted her if she'd been able to identify Wilson at the start of all of this? It had taken a lot for him to even consider Wilson could be involved.

If he couldn't trust Wilson, how could he trust anyone?

He trusted Jaycee though. That realization struck him. Had it only been a few days since they'd first met? Looking at her now, no one would suspect all she'd been through or that key pieces of her memory were missing. She kept herself calm and collected and was just as determined as he was to figure out who was behind all this mystery. She had to.

Her life and his reputation were at stake at the hands of someone who'd already proved to be ruthless.

Wilson had to be the one behind this. Brett couldn't deny it any longer.

His best friend and business partner, the man who'd watched his back for the past decade, was a killer.

It was time to confront Wilson once and for all and to put an end to this scheming. He wanted to look his friend in the eye and demand to know why.

Standing, he promised Hennessy that he would be in touch about what they found as he led Jaycee from the interview room and out to their car.

They raced to his office. He parked in the garage

then headed upstairs, using the back entrance, and made a beeline for Wilson's office. Brett jimmied the lock and let himself inside. Wilson was still out and his constant absence lately should give them plenty of time to discover any evidence in his office that he might be involved in Whitney's death or the plot to kill Jaycee.

Brett opened up his computer and his heart fell when he spotted the very same files Jaycee had copied.

He dug through Wilson's desk drawer and found a file folder containing more photos of Whitney, along with letters written to her, and invoices and payments made to Jaycee's company for security checks.

She glanced over his shoulder and sighed. "That's from my invoice company." She took one of the invoices and stared at it. "This matches the one I found on my computer. It's true. Wilson was the man who hired me."

Anger boiled through Brett at the betrayal as he stood and shoved everything off Wilson's desk in one fell swoop. He wasn't going to allow his so-called friend to get away with this.

"Calm down," Jaycee said, pulling him to her. She put her hands on his face. "Getting angry won't solve this."

"He was my best friend."

"I know."

She pressed her forehead against his and he held her, all the impulsive anger draining from him. She had a way of calming him that no one else could do. He touched her face then covered her mouth with his. She kissed him back. If he was going to stop denying things then he may as well stop denying his feelings for her. He'd fallen for her. She'd become more important to him than anyone else in his life.

"What's going on here?" Brett looked up to see Wilson standing in the doorway.

Brett pulled his gun and trained it on Wilson as he pushed Jaycee behind him.

It was time for a showdown and Brett would do whatever he had to do to keep the woman he loved safe.

Wilson dropped his briefcase onto the floor and raised his hands as Brett held the gun on him. "Whoa. What are you two doing in my office? And why do you have that gun pointed at me?"

"He hired you, didn't he?" Brett demanded. He wanted answers and he wanted them now. "Jack Milton, the producer. He hired you to kill Whitney."

Wilson's face registered shock. "I didn't kill anyone and I don't even know who Jack Milton is."

Brett moved around the desk to get closer to Wilson. "Then explain the large deposit of money into your bank account. Explain why you were shopping in the pricy electronics store and the motorcycle dealership today. Where'd that money come from, Wilson?"

"You looked into my bank account?"

"We sure did. That money was transferred to you from a private attorney's office."

Wilson shook his head. "It's not what you think, Brett. My great-uncle died a few months ago. He left me an inheritance. It just came through a few weeks ago."

"The day after Whitney was murdered. That's quite a coincidence."

Wilson blew out a breath. "Yes, it is, but it doesn't

make me a killer for hire. You've known me too long to believe that."

Brett grabbed the file from the desk. "Then explain this."

He took the file and opened it, his eyes widening as he stared at the images. He paled as he closed the file. "I've never seen these before."

"I just took that file from your desk, Wilson. And your computer has another file just like that. These seem to indicate that you were watching her."

"Brett, I don't even know where these images came from, but I didn't take them and I certainly didn't keep this file lying around for someone to find." He took a step back then looked from Jaycee to Brett. "You've been investigating me? Why?"

"I asked Jaycee to check into everyone here at the firm. It's obvious the attacks against her were coming from someone on the inside, so I had her go back through our personnel files. She found things that point to you. Also, Lincoln Albertson, the man the police have in custody, his plane ticket to Dallas was paid for with your company credit card. Someone brought him here to take the blame for Whitney's murder. That could only have been you."

Wilson's expression set. "I did not kill Whitney. I wouldn't do that, and I would never hurt Jaycee." He looked past Brett. "I promise you I didn't do anything to try to hurt you, Jaycee. I-I'm obviously being set up here."

Brett turned away from him, disgusted by the tactic. "Please, Wilson."

"No, you said it yourself. Someone inside this office is behind all of this. They're trying to place it all on me."

"Why would they do that?"

"Why would someone try to destroy your reputation? They're trying to ruin our business, Brett. Someone is trying to take us down. Listen to me, this is my business too. Why would I want to ruin the status of my own business? If I wanted to hurt you, I could have found another way to do so without taking down my own business. Come on, Brett. We've spent years building this place up. Why would I destroy that?"

Wilson's eyes pleaded with him for understanding and Brett wanted so much to believe him. He didn't want to think he'd been so blind to Wilson's nature. He looked into his friend's eyes and sighed. Wilson was right when he said he could have found a way to get to Brett that wouldn't harm the business. And he could have found a way around their security measures without having to hire Jaycee to do so. He had all the keys and codes in his possession. He wouldn't have needed outside help.

Mostly, Brett believed him because he trusted his friend and, by looking in Wilson's eyes, he saw the truth there.

He lowered his gun and nodded. "I believe you." He turned to Jaycee. "I believe him."

Wilson gave a relieved sigh and all the tension seemed to flow from his body. "Thank you." He lowered his hands then picked up his briefcase and set it on the chair. "Do you really believe someone in our office is behind this?"

Brett returned his gun to its holster. "Only someone inside could have gotten to Jaycee when her drink was spiked. This had to be an inside job. All indicators point to it."

Wilson thought for a moment then sighed. "I guess you're right. I just can't believe it. Besides me, was there anyone else on your radar?"

Brett turned to Jaycee, who stepped forward. "I found some inconsistencies with a couple of other people. Mitch Dearborn has gaps in his employment history. His previous employers have never heard of him."

That seemed to grab Wilson's attention. "I verified his references myself and they were all glowing recommendations."

"Or faked," Brett suggested.

"I guess so."

"And Sean Knight has gone missing under mysterious circumstances. We can't verify that he's with any legitimate missionary organization. But then again, if he's not been in the office, he couldn't have spiked my drink."

"Unless he's also working with someone else," Brett stated.

Wilson dragged his hand across his jaw as he considered everything she'd just said. "How did all this get past me?"

"Beat yourself up over it later," Brett told him. "For now, we need to figure out which one of these is behind this. We believe someone in this office got paid by this producer to target Jaycee. Whoever paid them probably killed Whitney too."

"What's going on?"

Brett pulled his gun and aimed it at the doorway and their sudden intruder.

Trish jumped and held up her hands. "It's only me! It's only me!"

"It's okay," Wilson said. "It's just Trish."

His pulse was still on fire as he lowered his weapon.

Jaycee touched his arm, reassuring him that everything was fine. But how had Trish gotten to the doorway without any of them realizing it?

"What is happening in here?" she demanded. "I didn't hear any of you come to the office and now you're all huddled in here being weird and pulling guns on me."

"We were just talking over some issues. What are you doing here on the weekend?"

"Just catching up on paperwork and, since you're back in the office, I have some forms I need you to sign."

"It can wait."

"Please, Wilson, they really need to go out today. If I messenger them, they can be there by Monday."

He sighed. "Fine." He turned to Brett and Jaycee. "I'll be right back."

Brett closed the office door behind them as they walked out. He turned to Jaycee. "We came in the back way. How did she know we were here?"

Jaycee shook her head. "She couldn't have heard us from her desk at the front. Does she have access to the back doors?"

"No. If we enter the code on the keypad, no one should be alerted that it's been opened."

"The office is closed today so it's quiet. Maybe she

really did just hear us." Even as she said it, he could tell she didn't believe it.

Jaycee turned to the desk and started feeling around the edges. He quickly realized what she was doing—looking for electronic listening devices. If someone was indeed attempting to frame Wilson for their misdeeds, they might have bugged his office.

Brett hurried to the bookcase and felt around too. His hand slid over a lamp and he felt something give. He sighed and pulled it off, turning to show her, then he dumped the device into the water jug of some fresh flowers.

"Someone's bugged Wilson's office," Jaycee said.

He nodded. "And I'm sure mine too."

"Do you think Trish is involved in this?"

"Somehow I don't see Trish having the sniper skills needed to shoot at us back at the ranch or at your apartment, but I can't say for sure she's not involved in some way. I think it's safe to say we need to take this conversation out of the office until we find out who placed this bug."

The door opened and Wilson reentered. "That was odd. Those papers she insisted I had to sign aren't due to be sent out until the first of the month."

"Maybe she realizes we're on to her." He pointed to the listening device in the jug of water.

He shook his head. "First someone tries to frame me for murder and now they're bugging my office. We have to figure out who is behind this, Brett."

"Let's start with Trish. If she's involved, I want to know about it."

They headed down the hallway to the front lobby. Trish's desk was empty.

"She was just here a minute ago," Wilson stated.

Brett heard someone approaching and instinctively reached for his gun. He noticed Wilson do the same. He hated that they had to be on guard in their own office, but until they knew who the enemy was, they had to be vigilant.

A figure emerged from around the corner. It was Mitch.

Brett turned to see Jaycee's eyes widen with fear and her face register recognition. She raised her hands to point to Mitch and cried out, "It's him! He's the one who tried to kill me!"

Brett spun back to Mitch who responded by pulling out his gun and firing at them.

# TEN

The memory that had been locked away came flooding back to Jaycee and she remembered the man so clearly. He was now standing in front of her. The man who'd hired her to breach Brett's systems then tried to murder her to shut her up. She'd seen his face in pictures but something about his gait and the curve of the smug smile on his face struck her. It was him.

Brett grabbed her and shoved her to the floor behind the desk as gunfire rained. He and Wilson, who'd also taken cover, fired back.

She saw through a slat on the reception desk that the man had also taken cover around the corner of the hallway.

Brett crouched down beside her and grabbed her shoulders. "Are you hit?"

Adrenaline was pulsing through her. She wasn't feeling any pain but she still checked herself. "No, I'm okay."

He glanced over at Wilson, who also indicated he was uninjured.

Memories were coming back to Jaycee faster than

she could even process them. Memories of her parents and their funeral, of being alone and how lonely she'd been since their deaths. Of meeting with the man now shooting at them and how charming he'd seemed at the time. Of discovering that someone had been murdered because of what she'd done.

She'd done her due diligence, confirming he'd worked for B&W before she'd taken the job, and now she knew the truth—that he'd been the one to confirm Joe Cleveland worked for B&W. Like Wilson, she'd been fooled by fake references. And she had given Harry Jackson from the bank's recommendation more weight than the others. Another falsehood she'd been duped by.

Mitch Dearborn had tricked her into becoming an accomplice to murder.

"Why does one of your people want me dead?" She knew Mitch was tying up loose ends by focusing on her, but what did this man have against Whitney or Brett in the first place? Why had he made her a target?

Brett shook his head. "I have no idea."

"You won't leave this office," Mitch called out to them. "None of you will for what you've done."

"What did we do, Mitch?" Brett asked him. "Why are you doing this?"

"You killed my brother. Now, you'll all pay!"

Brett checked his gun then looked at Jaycee. He leaned in. "According to Mitch's personnel file, he doesn't have a brother. We need to get somewhere safe out of his line of fire and figure this out. Now that we know who's targeting us, I want to know why."

Jaycee nodded. "If I can get to a computer, maybe I can use his personnel photo to do a reverse image search. If his references were faked, it's possible he's using a fake name."

"That's a good plan. The computer server room is in the back of the suite. If we can get there, we can access the internet."

"You go," Wilson told them. "I'll cover your getaway."

Brett took Jaycee's arm then, when Wilson motioned, he pulled her to her feet and pushed her toward the hallway that led to the computer server room. She heard shots being fired and covered her head as she ran, feeling Brett behind her, urging her along.

"What about Wilson?"

"He can take care of himself. I have to protect you. Go."

She hurried down the corridor. "There it is," he said pointing to a door at the end of the hallway. "That's the server room."

She pushed open the door and the cold from the air conditioner hit her. Server rooms had to be kept cooler than most other areas given the heat generated by the computers housed there.

She hurried to a monitor while Brett stood guard at the door.

"Hurry up. It won't be long before he comes looking for us."

As if in response to his words, gunfire sounded from down the hall.

Jaycee turned, suddenly worried that they'd trapped

themselves in a place they couldn't get out of. Brett opened the door to peek down the hall then closed it again and shook his head. "It wasn't near us. Probably Wilson trying to take him out."

She pulled up the employee files she'd accessed earlier and opened Mitch's file. His photo was inside. She copied and pasted that into the Google Image search engine and hit Return.

A photo popped up of Mitch Dearborn in his military uniform. Only, the name listed wasn't Mitch Dearborn. It was Saul Davenport.

Brett pushed up beside her. "Davenport?"

"Saul Davenport. Does the name ring a bell?"

He nodded but confusion colored his expression. "Tony Davenport was Whitney's fiancé."

"The one who served with you and Wilson in the marines?"

He nodded. "Saul must be his brother."

"But why would Tony's brother want to kill us?"

"I don't know. Revenge for not saving his brother?"

"Didn't you say you were at Tony's funeral? Why didn't you or Wilson recognize him from the funeral when you hired him?"

"No, he missed the funeral. He was overseas on a mission at the time. He was an army ranger and he was on assignment. Whitney said they weren't able to reach him until two weeks after Tony's funeral."

"So it's possible he blames you and Wilson for not saving his brother? But why kill Whitney if his brother loved her?"

"I don't know. But he took this job under false pretenses. He's been actively working against us. He might have even been the one to kill Whitney. We need to know why."

"We need to call the police," Jaycee told him. "There are other people in the building. They need to be cleared out in case Mitch—Saul—decides killing us is more important than innocent people's lives."

He nodded and pulled out his cell phone. "At least it's the weekend. The building won't be too occupied." He dialed then frowned when the call didn't go through. "He must have a cell phone jammer. We probably have some stored in the supply closet. It's possible he's using our own tech against us." Brett pounded his fist against the table. He picked up the landline on the wall but got only a beeping sound. No dial tone. "He's cut off our communications."

"Maybe I can send an email to building security. They can initiate evacuating the building and contacting the police." She quickly pulled up an email for security and typed a message, including the instructions to phone the police about an active shooter in the building. She also attached Mitch's photo so they would know who to look for.

She sent it off, praying they would see it.

"What do we do now?"

He checked his handgun. "We need more firepower if we're going to stop him. We have a storage room that houses our weapons supply. We need to get there."

"And let me guess, it's on the other end of the office."

He shrugged. "We didn't plan to be in a shootout when we chose it."

"Don't you think Mitch might be going there too?"

"It's secured with a code. Only Wilson and I have access. One of us has to approve any weapons checked out. He won't be able to get inside. However, if he's been behind this all this time, we have to assume he's prepared. Probably got weapons stashed in his office."

She hoped he was right that Mitch hadn't gone there. If she had to be locked in an office building with a shooter, she was glad Brett was there with her and knew how to protect her and himself.

He was on full alert as he opened the door and scanned the hallway. "It's clear. Let's move."

Brett walked in front of her as they hurried down the hallway and made a sharp turn. The office was a maze and she was again glad not to be alone with no way out and a madman hunting her.

She hadn't asked for this and it didn't involve her. Dearborn's grudge was against Brett and Wilson and Whitney. She could understand the grief of losing a brother as her own grief at losing her parents a few years ago came flooding back to her. But killing Whitney and hunting down Brett and Wilson? That, she didn't understand and wasn't sure she could unless he stopped chasing them long enough to explain himself.

*But why me, God?*

Brett would still be in this mess without her involvement, and Whitney might still be dead, but at least she would be safe and secure back at her apartment.

*And alone. Don't forget how alone you were then.*

Brett had been right about her when he'd said she'd trusted too much in herself. Her job gave her satisfaction because she was good at it and she loved the challenge, but she'd stood on her own for too long. She'd been able to be swayed by Mitch because she'd trusted herself more than she'd trusted anyone else.

Afraid to take a risk on people.

Afraid of being hurt.

Now look where that had gotten her.

Brett hurried toward a door with a keypad on the lock. He quickly typed in a number then tried the knob.

Nothing happened.

He keyed in the number again and tried the knob. It didn't budge.

"Something's wrong. No one else should have access to this, but my code isn't working."

"Who else could have changed it?"

"Only Wilson…"

Were they back to suspecting Wilson again?

He glanced at her as realization hit his face. "Or Trish."

Trish. Of course. They'd suspected she might be involved and Jaycee remembered her telling her that she had backups for all the keys and codes in the office. Another trusted employee who'd betrayed them.

"Stand back," he instructed Jaycee.

She moved away from the door as he kicked it several times before the door slammed open. He ushered Jaycee inside and secured the door closed as quickly as possible.

He breathed a sigh of relief at seeing the weapons were still there. Mitch hadn't been here yet, though he'd made sure to try to lock them out.

Brett grabbed another handgun and several clips and stuffed them into his pockets. He also reached for a rifle and made sure it was loaded before he turned to Jaycee. "I've got to get you out of this building."

The thought of leaving him overwhelmed her. "I don't want to go without you." The possibility of him confronting Mitch and not coming back suddenly filled her with dread. He would put his life at risk to keep her safe but she didn't want to leave his side.

He touched her face. "Once you're safe, I need to end this with Mitch. Whatever his beef is with us, I can't allow him to continue hurting people. He killed Whitney and he tried to kill you."

"Come with me. Let the police handle Mitch." It was an empty request. She knew Brett couldn't let that happen. People were in danger—she was in danger—because of someone in his employment.

He couldn't let it go.

She didn't want to lose him without letting him know how much she cared about him. "Brett, I know you said you didn't want to act on this attraction between us, but I don't want this to end without telling you this." She took a deep breath. "I've fallen for you, Brett Harmon."

His eyes roamed her face as he soaked in her words, but she could see he was still holding back. "Jaycee..."

"I know but I don't care. My memories are back. I remember everything and I'm in love with you." She closed the distance between them and kissed him.

Brett's heart raced from the lingering smell of Jaycee's shampoo. He'd tried to hold back his attraction to her but holding her, feeling her lips on his, it felt right. He returned her kiss, loving the way she gave in to him.

Only movement outside pulled his attention away from her.

He raised his gun at the beep-beep sound of someone using the keypad. It didn't work for that person either.

Brett pushed her behind him, bracing himself for whoever was about to come through that door. He'd allowed someone to get close to her again. Mistake. He gulped. He couldn't call kissing her a mistake though.

He shook off that thought as something scratched at the door. He would shoot whoever came through that door if it meant keeping her safe.

The door burst open and Wilson fell into the room.

Brett breathed a sigh of relief and lowered his weapon. He closed the door behind Wilson and secured it again.

"Are you okay?"

Wilson nodded but looked from Brett to Jaycee. "Everything okay in here?"

He felt his face warm. Could he know about that kiss? She'd caught him off guard but he couldn't say he regretted it. He'd been wanting to kiss her since that moment at the ranch.

"We're fine," he told Wilson. "What happened?"

"I emptied my clip trying to get away from him. He's got the place locked down. The outside doors are chained up."

"He also tried to lock us out of the weapons room. My code didn't work. That's why I had to break in."

Wilson thought for a moment then grimaced. "Trish.

She's the only other person who could have changed the code."

Brett nodded. "That's what we were thinking. She's probably the one who spiked Jaycee's drink too. She would have known which was hers."

Wilson heaved an infuriated sigh, his frustration obvious. "Why would Trish be working with Mitch? For that matter, why would Mitch be shooting at us?"

"I don't know about Trish but Jaycee did a facial search with his personnel file. Mitch Dearborn is a fake identity. He's really Saul Davenport, Tony Davenport's army ranger older brother."

Wilson's eyes widened. "Tony's brother?"

"And Whitney's fiancé's brother. I still don't know why he wanted her dead or why he took a job here under a fake name. Maybe he thought that was the easiest way to get to Whitney but discovered he couldn't so he hired Jaycee to get close to her. And he would have known about the letters Albertson sent her since he was part of the team investigating the grudge list she gave us. He made Lincoln Albertson his fall guy." Exasperation rattled through Brett. It seemed the more answers they uncovered, the more questions they raised. "Truthfully, I don't know anything except that I have to get Jaycee out of his line of fire."

"Mitch is jamming the phone signals, too, so we can't even get a message in or out to alert the police. I tried pulling the fire alarm too. Nothing. He must have disabled it."

"Jaycee was able to send an email to building security, but we have no way of knowing if they received it."

"I haven't heard any sirens. Looks like we're trapped in here."

Brett shook his head. "I have to get Jaycee to safety. We've got to find a way out." He wasn't taking any more risks with her life. He and Wilson could deal with Mitch and whatever was going on with him later.

Her safety was his top priority.

Jaycee picked out a handgun from their supplies and made sure it was loaded and ready to go. Brett gave her an amused look but she wasn't going out there again without a way to defend herself.

"I took a class," she told him. "I've never fired one, but I will if I have to." Now that her memories had returned, she recalled everything her instructor had taught her about handling a weapon.

Only, this wasn't the gun she'd learned on. That was sitting in an evidence locker back in Jessup.

Brett didn't try to talk her out of arming herself. He quickly showed her how to use this model. "Keep it with you but don't fire unless it's necessary."

She understood his meaning. He planned to protect her, so she shouldn't need a weapon, but they both knew better than anyone that even the best laid plans got changed.

Wilson stood at the door. "Your best chance is to get to the front doors and exit there any way you can. I'll take the west hallway. Maybe I can cut Mitch off so you two can get out."

Brett picked up his own weapon. "I'm sending Jaycee out, then I'm coming back in. She can call for help but I want her away from the line of fire."

"You don't have to come back in, Brett. Get her to safety."

He shook his head. "I can't do that. Mitch has been outed. His fake identity is burned. He's not going to stop until he gets what he wants."

"Great," Wilson stated. "Anybody know what that is? I guess his plan is just to kill us all?"

Brett shrugged but Jaycee thought Wilson might be right. Somehow, they and Whitney had wronged him, at least in his mind. He'd already killed Whitney. He wouldn't hesitate to kill them too.

Brett and Wilson clasped hands. "Take care," Wilson told him before he pulled open the door and rushed from the room. He took off down the hallway.

Brett raised his gun and motioned for Jaycee to follow him. She gripped the weapon in her hand and did so, on guard for every step of the way. They headed toward the front of the building, past the hallway of offices and the conference room. When she saw it, she knew where she was. Almost dying in a room helped cement its location in her mind.

Brett motioned for her to wait as he checked behind the reception desk then around the other corner where Mitch had first started shooting. Once it was all clear, he ran to the entrance doors that led into the foyer. A chain with a padlock prevented them from opening.

"We'll have to bust through the door."

"Can you shoot the lock?" she asked him. She'd seen that happen on TV shows.

He grabbed the lock then the chain and shook his head. "It's a heavy-duty steel lock. Maybe if I had more time I could—"

Jaycee spotted movement around the corner. "Watch out," she hollered as Mitch appeared and started firing.

She took off running while Brett dove for cover, returning Mitch's fire. Jaycee ran into the kitchen and crouched on the floor. Her heart was racing as she dared to peek around the corner. Brett was pinned down. She couldn't leave him or Mitch would surely kill him.

She clutched the gun in her hand then jumped up and fired off several shots.

They all went wide and slammed against the walls, but Mitch turned to her and, when he did, Brett took the opportunity to tackle him, knocking him off his feet.

"Run!" He yelled the command at Jaycee as he charged again at Mitch.

She turned and took off down the hallway, the sound of gunfire ringing in her ears. She stopped only when she realized the shooting had stopped. She slid against the wall to catch her breath, praying for Brett to appear around that corner.

No one came.

She was alone.

Brett would surely have followed behind her if he was able to and each second that he didn't appear ripped through her. Hot tears burned her eyes. She didn't know if he was alive or dead and she didn't dare go back to look.

She had to keep going. She had to get to safety.

*Oh God, please help me find my way out of here.*

She wasn't ready to die and she was determined to find help and bring it back to Brett.

She ran down the long corridor and came to another hallway. This place was a maze and she didn't know her way around it. She didn't even want to think about the advantage that gave her assailant.

Relief flooded her when she spotted the exit sign and the back door. It wasn't chained, but when she tried the door handle, it didn't move. She wasn't going to let that stop her.

She set down her gun and grabbed the fire extinguisher off the wall. She slammed it down hard on the handle over and over until she felt it give and break. Relief flooded her as she pushed open the door and stumbled into the foyer where the elevator and stairway access to the garage were.

She pulled open the staircase door and hurried down the steps. She'd gotten separated from Brett but she still heard gunfire in the building. She had to get to the lower level and find some help.

She grabbed hold of the railing as she quickly descended.

Above her, a door slammed shut. She stopped cold at the sound. She gazed up and saw a face staring down at her.

Mitch!

He aimed his gun and fired. She screamed and took off running as the bullets pinged the metal.

She burst through the next access door. She had to get out of the stairwell before she was hit by bullets ping-ponging everywhere. On the third floor were office doors. She pushed them but they were locked.

She opened the stairwell door again. She had no choice but to keep searching for a safe exit. Only, she heard footsteps so closely heading downward.

Jaycee shut the door behind her, her panic rising as she realized the elevator was her only chance to escape. It was only a garage access but if she could get to the bottom level while he was still searching, she might be able to get away and call for help. But if he saw what she was doing, she would be trapped inside.

Anxiety filled her as the doors slid open and a moment of paralyzing fear swept through her. She fought back against it. She had to do this. Her life, Brett's life, even Wilson's life, depended on getting help.

She forced herself inside and jabbed the ground level button. She pressed her back against the side so she could see when the doors opened and tried not to think about the dread building in her chest.

She suddenly realized she'd left her gun upstairs when she'd grabbed the fire extinguisher. Stupid, stupid. Now she had no way to defend herself.

Tears pressed against her eyes. Where was Brett? He would surely have come to find her if he was able. Did that mean he was dead? Had Mitch shot him while she'd run away?

She couldn't think like that. She hadn't stopped running, so, of course, Brett couldn't catch up with her.

The elevator glided to the bottom level and dinged as the doors slid open. She peeked around the corner through the open doorway. No one was in sight.

Good. This was her chance to escape.

She hurried out and heard the squeal of tires.

Jaycee glanced up to see Trish behind the wheel of a car heading right for her.

She ran but Trish turned the car and rammed into her. Jaycee hit the front grill then rolled over the hood, slamming to the ground as Trish hit the brakes.

Pain radiated through Jaycee's leg. She would be surprised if it wasn't broken, but she knew she wasn't going to be able to run on it.

The car door opened and Trish hopped out and ran over to her. Jaycee stared up to see her holding a gun aimed right at her.

# ELEVEN

"You're not going anywhere," Trish told her, a smug smile forming on her face.

Jaycee pushed away the nausea that rolled through her at the pain in her leg. She didn't know Trish that well but she'd already realized it must have been her who'd spiked her drink with antifreeze.

If she was capable of doing that to Jaycee then she was capable of anything.

"You're working with Mitch? I thought you cared about Brett and Wilson."

"I did until I learned what they did to Mitch's brother."

"That's not even his name. Did he tell you that?"

"He told me everything. They let his brother just die in that explosion. They left him to die and didn't do anything to help him."

Brett had never told her the exact details of the battle in which Tony was killed, but she knew him well enough to doubt that story. "I know Mitch might believe it happened like that, but you know Brett isn't capable of leaving someone behind. It's not his way."

"You don't even know them. How could you know what they're like? I've known them both for a lot longer than you."

"Then you should be ashamed of yourself," Jaycee insisted. "If you really knew them, you would know they weren't capable of what you're claiming or of what Mitch—or whatever his name is—is claiming. Brett is a good man. He cares about you and he cares about this business and helping people. People like me and Whitney." Suddenly a thought hit her. "I suppose you think her death was justified too?"

Her face grimaced and hardened. "She got what she deserved."

"She deserved to die? Is that what Mitch's brother would have wanted? He loved her. He was going to marry her."

"And she forgot about him the moment he was in the ground. She went off and became a celebrity within four months of his death. Did you know that? She didn't give him a second thought."

Jaycee could see that Trish had eaten up every word Mitch had told her. "That's not true. Brett told me that she loved him. She talked about him all the time. He told me so."

"He'll say anything to justify his guilt."

Jaycee chuckled at that. "And you'll believe anything to justify yours. How did he convince you, Trish? Was it just his tale of woe or did he offer you something too? Money? Romance?"

Trish shifted uncomfortably and Jaycee knew she'd

hit on the reason behind all of this. She couldn't help but laugh. "You think he's in love with you?"

"I don't want his money but, yes, we are in love. I fell for his sympathetic story the moment I heard him. I admire him for standing up for his brother when no one else did."

Jaycee recalled Brett telling her that Trish's cousin had been killed by her husband and that Trish had been so angry because no one had stepped in to help her. Mitch had been smart to target her weak spot with his story of woe.

Trish motioned toward the elevator. "Let's go."

Jaycee shook her head. There was no way she could make it back upstairs. "You hurt my leg. I can't walk."

Trish looked at her as if she was lying, but finally sighed and pulled out a hand-held radio. She pressed the button and spoke into it. "I've got Jaycee but I had to hit her with my car. She can't move."

The voice that responded to her sounded sinister to Jaycee's ears. "I'm on my way to you. Keep her there."

It saddened Jaycee to think how easily Trish had been fooled by someone else's dark tale. They had that in common. She, too, had fallen for Mitch's tale. She'd believed him enough to break into B&W Security and bring down their systems.

But she hadn't actively participated in deception or tried to kill another person. That was where their similarities ended.

Trish would stand by while Mitch killed everyone all to avenge his brother's death.

She couldn't just sit here and wait for him to come and shoot her. She had to at least fight back.

First, she had to get away from Trish.

Trish's gaze darted from her to the stairway door and back to her again. If Jaycee could distract her long enough, she might be able to escape. It wasn't going to be easy, especially with her leg, but she wasn't going to just let herself get shot.

Determination settled inside her. This was the woman who'd poisoned her drink with antifreeze and possibly locked her inside a running car—that might have been Mitch, but she'd at least let him know she was going to the garage—then run her over with one. If Jaycee was going down, she was going down fighting.

Jaycee grabbed her leg and cried out, causing Trish to move closer to her. "Don't worry. It'll be over once Mitch gets here." Her gaze darted to the stairwell door again.

Jaycee took her shot.

With her good leg, she kicked Trish and brought her to her knees. She grabbed for the gun and struggled, fighting through the pain that ravaged her until she whipped the gun from Trish's hand and slammed it into her face.

Trish went down.

Jaycee climbed to her feet, ignoring the pain that threatened her, and hobbled toward the elevator, hyperaware that the stairwell door could open at any moment and Mitch could grab her. She had to get out of there before that happened.

She pressed the elevator button and the doors slid open. Trish started moving and moaning on the ground just as they slid shut.

Jaycee hit a random button. She had nowhere to go,

but she needed to put some distance between them and her. If she could reach one of the other offices in the building, maybe she could find a phone to call for help. And she had to do it before Mitch and Trish figured out where she'd gone.

The elevator slid to a stop on the fifth floor and the doors opened. She peeked around the corner. No one was in the entryway for this floor and she spotted a Juliet balcony at the end. Maybe she could call down to the street for someone to help. Why weren't the police there yet? She was certain someone had to have heard the gunfire. Then again, it was the weekend and the building was nearly empty as were the downtown streets.

She hurried to the balcony and pulled open the doors. She leaned over, trying to get a look at the street below. No one was in sight. What she wouldn't give for a group of paparazzi right about now. But would they even stop shouting questions or taking photos long enough to call for help?

Suddenly, the stairway door slammed open. Jaycee ran back toward the elevator, but it was too late. Mitch blocked her way, grabbing her and shoving her against the wall. "Did you think you could escape me again, Jaycee?"

Trish appeared behind him and kicked Jaycee's injured leg. She cried out at the pain that ripped through her.

"You're more tenacious than I expected," Mitch told her.

"Sorry to disappoint you." Fear pulsed through her along with the pain but Jaycee wouldn't give him the satisfaction of seeing her plead for her life. She wouldn't go out that way.

She didn't know what had happened to Brett, if he was alive or dead, but she knew in that instant that she wasn't alone. God was with her, giving her the strength to face down whatever Mitch did to her.

He'd already tried to kill her several times. This time, this close, it was unlikely he would fail. She was going to die here.

Brett skirted down the long hallway that led to the back entrance. He'd gotten away from Mitch by the seat of his pants and had been searching for Jaycee ever since. He hoped she'd gotten away but the lack of police sirens outside told him that was unlikely.

He had to find her.

Mitch had to have been planning this for who knew how long. He wasn't going to fall down on the job now, not when he was so close to the end of his mission of ruining their lives and killing everyone he blamed for his brother's death. Or, at least, he assumed that was his grudge against them. He hadn't stopped to explain his plan.

Brett had been impressed by his background and skill set when they'd interviewed Mitch for the job at B&W. His résumé had boasted that he'd been a former special ops ranger for many years. At least, that had been the truth.

He recalled Tony commenting on how proud his big brother had been when he joined the marines. Tony had been proud of his army ranger brother, only Brett wondered what his kid brother would think of him now. Tony Davenport had been a good man and a good marine. He would never have approved of his brother's behavior and Brett knew he would be heartbroken to see how far his brother had fallen.

Brett hated to be the one to take Mitch down, but he would do anything to protect Jaycee.

He heard gunfire in the hallway and headed toward the sound. He prayed Jaycee had taken cover somewhere and was safe and hiding, but he couldn't depend on that. He still didn't understand how they'd become so separated but he couldn't think on that now. All he could think about was getting to her and rescuing her.

*God, please keep her safe until I can reach her. I can't lose her.*

She'd become too important to him and he hadn't even told her. He needed to tell her. He was impressed with her bravery and her determination. He'd fallen head over heels for her. He'd never known he could care so much about another person. He'd always done his best to keep people at arm's length. His stepdad used to say it was how he protected himself from getting hurt, and he'd been right. He'd lost his dad then his mom. Without his stepdad, he would have been totally alone in the world or worse…left to his grandfather to raise.

He knew from his stepdad that his grandfather had tried to take custody of him but Brett had been old enough to decide for himself where he'd wanted to live and he'd told a judge so. He hadn't known at the time the battle his stepdad had gone through to keep him with him, but he was thankful. He didn't know what kind of man he might have become being raised by someone so full of anger and bitterness.

Charlie was a good man and Brett had been blessed to have him in his life. He would be glad to know that he wasn't holding anyone at arm's length any longer. He wanted to be with Jaycee. He could see a future with her, a family and a life of happiness stretched out before him.

All he had to do was keep her alive long enough to claim it.

He pushed open a door and cleared each room as he made his way down the hallway. He prayed with each door that he would find her hiding inside and, each time, he was disappointed.

He approached the back entrance door. It stood open. That was good news. She must have gone out that way. At least, he hoped she had. And that Mitch hadn't followed her.

He approached the door and raised his guard as he stepped through.

The foyer was empty.

Voices grabbed his attention. He opened the stairwell door and heard them float up to him. Quietly, he made his way down a flight of stairs.

His heart leapt when he heard Jaycee's voice coming from the fifth floor. She sounded frightened, but she was alive. He peeked through a window on the stairwell door and saw her, Mitch and Trish all converged in the foyer. Mitch had her pinned against the wall but she wasn't cowering to him.

"You shouldn't have come after me. You pulled me

into a murder plot. You didn't really expect me to keep quiet about that, did you?"

Brett grinned at the bite in her voice. *Way to clap back, Jaycee.*

Mitch laughed at her spunk. "No, I didn't. I always intended to kill you. I even went to find you at your apartment the day after I killed Whitney but you were gone. There was no sign of you. I thought maybe you'd figured out what had happened and had the good sense to run. It wasn't until you showed up here asking questions and looking for Brett that I realized you were digging into what happened. You should have stayed gone, Jaycee. You were the perfect mark with no outside contacts and no family. You were all alone and perfect for my needs."

Brett gripped his weapon and reacted. He couldn't lose her now. He pushed through the door and stepped into the foyer, his gun trained at Mitch. "She's not alone anymore."

Mitch spun them both around then pulled Jaycee against him to use as a shield as Brett stood at the other end of the entryway, gun raised and ready to fight.

"Let her go and let's you and me deal with this."

But Mitch wasn't backing down. "That's not going to happen."

"What was your plan, Mitch? Or should I say Saul? You murdered Whitney. You plotted against me and Wilson and even Jaycee. You lured Trish into doing your bidding. Is this what your brother would have wanted from you, Mitch? I knew him and I know for a fact he wouldn't have wanted this. He was proud of you. He talked about you all the time. All he wanted to do was to live up to your expectations."

"And you let him die." His retort was hard and angry. He dug the gun into Jaycee's temple, causing her to cry out in pain.

"The enemy killed him, not me. Wilson and I and the rest of the squad did what we could to try to save him. We fought for him but it was too late. We couldn't save him."

"You should have tried harder!" He was losing control fast.

Behind Brett, the stairwell door opened and Wilson entered, gun at the ready. "Sorry I'm late for the party. I managed to get into one of the other offices and called the police. They're on their way."

"You can't get away now," Brett told Mitch. "Just let her go and we can talk this out."

"There's nothing to talk about!" Mitch shouted again. "Whitney got what she deserved. She claimed to love my brother then moved on after he died. And you and Wilson deserved to pay too."

The entryway was too narrow to try to get past him. Jaycee tried to go limp but Mitch kept her tightly on her feet. In fact, she was on her tiptoes trying to keep him from strangling her. She was trapped. So was Mitch, and he knew it. That made him even more dangerous.

He took several steps back but they were blocked in by the Juliette balcony. Mitch was trapped, but Brett felt it in his bones that he wasn't going to surrender quietly. He wanted to make everyone in this room pay for his brother's death.

"Let her go," Brett said again, doing his best to hide the quiver of panic he felt. He saw worry fill Jaycee's eyes. He hadn't done a good enough job. She knew him so well. On the outside, he was the cool and collected marine who didn't get rattled. He'd faced down bad guys with a lot more weaponry than Mitch possessed, but he'd never been as personally vested in the outcome as he was at this moment.

Mitch was holding Brett's future in his hands and threatening to end it.

Each step Brett took, Mitch stepped backward. They were running out of space and their silent standoff was loud with intentions.

Trish had enough. She raised her gun and fired off a couple of shots at Brett. Wilson fired back, hitting her in the shoulder and sending her to the ground. Brett didn't take his eyes off Mitch. He used that distraction to fire, too, and pulled the trigger. His bullet was dead-on, missing Jaycee and hitting Mitch instead.

He doubled over then jerked upright, sending Jaycee off balance. Her leg buckled beneath her and she stumbled backward. So did Mitch, but with greater force, hitting the Juliette balcony rail and losing his balance. He tumbled over it and, to Brett's horror, pulled Jaycee over with him.

Her scream ripped at his heart. He raced for the balcony, relief filling him when he saw Jaycee clinging to the railing for dear life.

But Mitch was hanging on to her, pulling and tugging, trying to climb his way over her.

Brett braced himself. He was not letting this maniac take Jaycee down with him.

"Help me," she cried, hanging on with one hand and being pulled with the other. Her fingers were slipping and it was only a matter of time before they both fell to the concrete sidewalk below.

Brett climbed over the edge, bracing himself to pull Jaycee up to safety. Mitch saw what he was doing and raised the gun in his free hand. Brett didn't hesitate. He fired first.

Mitch's hand lost its grip on Jaycee's arm and he hit the ground below.

All Brett's attention turned to making sure that didn't happen to her too. "Jaycee, give me your hand."

Sweat poured off her. She was losing her grip on the railing but Brett grabbed her arm. "I'm going to pull you up," he told her. "Give me your other hand."

She slung her shoulder and he grabbed her arm and clung to it just as her other hand slipped.

"I've got you," he told her. Wilson joined him at the balcony and together they hefted her up and over the railing.

Jaycee fell into his arms and they both tumbled to the floor. He didn't bother trying to get up and neither did she. He was vaguely aware of Wilson binding Trish's hands with a plastic zip tie.

Brett touched her face, his eyes soaking her in and gratitude rushing through him. Emotion overwhelmed him. "I thought I'd lost you."

"You nearly did."

He pulled his hand through her hair. "I'll never let you go again," he promised and then kissed her.

She broke the kiss and locked eyes with him, and his heart skipped a beat.

"What's wrong?"

"Trish bought into Mitch's story and so did I. How can you forgive me and not her?"

Relief flooded him. She had no reason to be worried about that anymore. "She chose to believe a lie and chose to act on it. You didn't do that."

"So you forgive me?"

"No, Jaycee. I don't blame you, so there's nothing to forgive. In fact, if it wasn't for you, I might never have known who was behind this. I do have a question for you though. Mitch said you disappeared right after Whitney's murder. Where did you go and why did you wait so long to come find me?"

It had all come back to her now. "The day after I did the job for him, I took a sabbatical. I'd been so unhappy with the way my life was headed and how lonely I was. I wanted some time to pray and try to figure out how to make changes in my life, how to make it better. I turned off my phone. There was no TV. No computer. I didn't even know what had happened until I returned home."

"And what did you decide on that sabbatical?"

She smiled. "I realized that my life was in God's hands. That He would lead me wherever I needed to be. I remember feeling a peace that everything was going to be okay. Then I returned home to find myself embroiled in murder."

His heart broke for what she'd been through. She

hadn't deserved any of it. "I'm so sorry you got pulled into it."

"I'm not. It brought me to you." She kissed him again and he soaked in her embrace. He was never letting her go again.

Brett stared at the headline running across his phone's screen as he sat in the kitchen at Harmon Ranch. Lincoln Albertson had been released and his name cleared in Whitney's death. Trish had been arrested for her role in Mitch's, aka Saul's, scheme and with him now dead, she was shouldering most of the blame in the media.

He felt sorry for her and the lies she'd believed. Mitch could never have pulled off his revenge plan without her assistance and now she would have to pay for her part.

Brett shut off his phone. He'd had enough news coverage to last him a lifetime. He was ready to move on from it and get on with his life. A life that included rebuilding his security business.

Caleb and Luke entered the kitchen. "Did you sign them?" Caleb asked.

Brett nodded and slid the stack of papers toward him that cemented his share of the inheritance of Harmon Ranch.

Luke grinned. "You deserve it. We all do."

"I can drop these off at the lawyer's office for you if you'd like," Caleb offered.

Brett stood and pulled on his jacket. "I'd appreciate that." He'd talked to his cousins and ultimately decided not to sell his quarter of the ranch. He wasn't ready to live here yet—he still had a life in Dallas—but this place would always be home to him.

And he wasn't yet ready to say goodbye to his cousins for good again either.

He shook Caleb's hand then Luke's.

"Don't be a stranger," Luke told him.

Brett smiled. "Don't worry. I won't be."

He walked out to his Charger, which had been repaired, and started the engine, smiling as he exited beneath the Harmon Ranch sign and headed for the highway to return to Dallas.

Harmon Ranch belonged to his past and possibly to his distant future, but it would be here waiting for him when he was ready.

Besides, he had a much more pressing future that he couldn't wait to get back to.

*Jaycee.*

Jaycee settled into her apartment. Her leg still ached but at least it hadn't been broken when Trish had hit her with her car. Brett had asked her to go to the ranch with him, but she'd wanted to get her apartment cleaned up. With all the danger out of their lives, she was ready to put things back in order.

So far, this place felt like home again in a way. She remembered being here, living here, and also how lonely she'd been. Now that she and Brett were in love, she didn't plan on being lonely ever again.

A knock on the door drew her attention. She hurried to answer it. Brett stood there, looking so handsome in a suit and tie. He cleaned up good and she liked this look on him.

He handed her a bouquet of flowers then gave her a soft kiss. She sank into it, basking in the headiness of this new relationship. Everything about her life had been turned upside down but had been set straight now, except her business. She wasn't sure what she was going to do about it, but she was certain she couldn't go on like she had been, vetting clients on her own. Trying to do things herself had gotten them all into a world of hurt.

"How is everything at B&W?"

It had been more than a week since the shootout with Mitch. "We're putting the office back together. We hired a new receptionist today. Wilson and I both made certain she wasn't the homicidal type as far as we can tell."

She saw it still pained him to think about Trish's betrayal. She'd claimed to be tricked, but she'd done just as she'd wanted to do. Trish had closed her eyes to the truth and followed deception down a dark path.

Jaycee poured them both a glass of iced tea and handed one to Brett. He took it and sipped.

"I also have news about Harry Jackson. He confessed to embezzling from First United and agreed to probation as long as he gets counseling for his gambling addiction in addition to paying the bank back for what he took."

She held no ill will for Harry. At least he hadn't fallen for Mitch, or Saul's, charms. He'd been bullied and blackmailed, getting a first-hand view of his dark side. Now that she'd seen it too, she had some sympathy for him.

"I'm glad. Let me put these flowers into some water,"

she told him. She hurried into the kitchen, found a vase for the flowers and filled it with water.

"I have something I want to ask you, Jaycee. It's important."

Her heart raced with anticipation. He was going to propose. She finished filling the vase but didn't dare lift it from the sink for fear she might drop it and shatter it.

"Jaycee?"

She turned to him and stared up into his face. She was ready to stop being alone and bask in what it felt like to be loved and to understand how amazing that was. There was no doubt in her mind that she would accept him.

"I need to ask you a question."

She held her breath as he reached into his jacket and pulled something out. Only, instead of a ring, he handed her a manila envelope.

"What's this?"

"Open it."

She pulled at the tabs and tore into it, pulling out a set of papers with her name and his.

And Wilson's?

It was a contract.

"Wilson and I talked about it. We would like to offer you a job with us at B&W. You'd be a great asset to our company."

She let out her breath, a little disappointed. She'd been expecting a proposal, not a job offer.

Yet the thought of not working alone again was intriguing. She smiled, realizing this was just the thing she'd been hoping for moments ago. "I think coming to work with you and Wilson is a great idea. I would love that. Thank you. I'll look this contract over and return it to you."

She turned back to the flowers. Her heart was hammering but she was doing her best to keep cool and steady. He hadn't offered her everything she'd wanted but it was a good place to start.

She placed the flowers into the vase then picked it up and turned to carry it to the living room. Brett still stood behind her, only this time in his hand, he held a ring box.

"Now that business is out of the way, I have one more question for you."

The vase slipped from her hand and hit the floor, shattering.

Brett yanked her from the spray of water and jarring edges. "I didn't mean to startle you."

She didn't care about the floor or the flowers or the shards of glass. "You didn't." The choke in her voice was nearly enough to make her start crying, which she did when Brett pulled her away from the broken glass and into the living room then removed the ring from the box and knelt before her.

"Jaycee Richmond, I want you to be my partner in business but, more than that, I want you to be my partner in life. I've never met anyone as strong and courageous and kind as you are. I've fallen head over heels in love with you, Jaycee. Will you marry me?"

The tears broke into a smile and she nodded. "Yes, of course, I will marry you, Brett."

He slipped the ring on her finger and stood. She

leaned in and kissed him. "I love you. Thank you for finding me and bringing me home."

She would be a part of the Harmon family and a partner in a marriage and a business.

She would never be lonely again.

*****

*If you enjoyed this Cowboy Protectors novel, be sure to pick up the previous book in this series by Virginia Vaughan:*

Kidnapped in Texas

*Available now from Love Inspired Suspense!*

Dear Reader,

Starting a new series is always fun. Getting to know new characters and learning about their quirks and their lives is great. But what happens if your character doesn't even know those things? That's the situation my heroine, Jaycee, finds herself in after being attacked. She doesn't remember anything about herself, not even her own name! And the more she discovers about her life, the more she wishes she could forget.

Thank you for getting to know Jaycee and Brett right along with me! I look forward to meeting and learning about more characters in my Cowboy Protectors series. I hope you'll join me.

I love to hear from my readers! Please keep in touch. You can reach me online at my website www.virginiavaughanonline.com or follow me on Facebook at www.Facebook.com/ginvaughanbooks.

Blessings!
*Virginia*

## COMING NEXT MONTH FROM
## **Love Inspired Suspense**

### EXPLOSIVE TRAIL
*Pacific Northwest K-9 Unit* • by Terri Reed

Hospitalized after an explosion in Olympic National Park, K-9 officer Willow Bates needs her estranged husband's help to stop the serial bomber. FBI agent Theo Bates is determined to keep his family safe—especially after learning he's about to become a father. But can they outwit a killer with an explosive agenda?

### DEADLY AMISH ABDUCTION
by Laura Scott

After witnessing a murder outside of her café, Rachel Miller runs for her life and turns to Amish farmer Jacob Strauss for protection. After evading several kidnapping attempts, she realizes the danger may be linked to her past—but searching for hidden truths could prove deadly.

### MONTANA COLD CASE CONSPIRACY
by Sharon Dunn

When new evidence from her father's cold-case disappearance surfaces, Lila Christie returns to town to unravel the mystery. But someone will do anything to keep her from uncovering secrets. She'll need help from her ex-fiancé, Sheriff Stewart Duncan, to find answers without losing her life.

### TRACKING THE TINY TARGET
by Connie Queen

Bristol Delaney will search every inch of Texas to find her kidnapped three-year-old son—even with someone dead set on stopping her. Can deputy sheriff Chandler Murphy and his search-and-rescue dog help her locate her little boy while safeguarding her...before it's too late?

### ELIMINATING THE WITNESS
by Jordyn Redwood

Testifying against her serial killer ex-husband put a target on Rachel Bright's back, and when he's released from prison, Rachel's identity in witness protection is exposed. Now she and US Marshal Kyle Reid must go on the run...but can Kyle protect Rachel before she becomes another victim?

### COUGAR MOUNTAIN AMBUSH
by Kathie Ridings

When game warden Carrie Caldwell is working on his family's ranch, the last thing Dr. Thad Hanson expects is for her to be threatened by a sniper. Now they'll have to work together to stay alive before falling prey to a killer out for revenge.

---

**LOOK FOR THESE AND OTHER LOVE INSPIRED BOOKS WHEREVER BOOKS ARE SOLD, INCLUDING MOST BOOKSTORES, SUPERMARKETS, DISCOUNT STORES AND DRUGSTORES.**

LISCNM0423

# Get 4 FREE REWARDS!

**We'll send you 2 FREE Books plus 2 FREE Mystery Gifts.**

Both the **Love Inspired®** and **Love Inspired® Suspense** series feature compelling novels filled with inspirational romance, faith, forgiveness and hope.

**YES!** Please send me 2 FREE novels from the Love Inspired or Love Inspired Suspense series and my 2 FREE gifts (gifts are worth about $10 retail). After receiving them, if I don't wish to receive any more books, I can return the shipping statement marked "cancel." If I don't cancel, I will receive 6 brand-new Love Inspired Larger-Print books or Love Inspired Suspense Larger-Print books every month and be billed just $6.49 each in the U.S. or $6.74 each in Canada. That is a savings of at least 16% off the cover price. It's quite a bargain! Shipping and handling is just 50¢ per book in the U.S. and $1.25 per book in Canada.* I understand that accepting the 2 free books and gifts places me under no obligation to buy anything. I can always return a shipment and cancel at any time by calling the number below. The free books and gifts are mine to keep no matter what I decide.

Choose one: ☐ **Love Inspired Larger-Print** (122/322 IDN GRHK) ☐ **Love Inspired Suspense Larger-Print** (107/307 IDN GRHK)

Name (please print)

Address Apt. #

City State/Province Zip/Postal Code

**Email:** Please check this box ☐ if you would like to receive newsletters and promotional emails from Harlequin Enterprises ULC and its affiliates. You can unsubscribe anytime.

Mail to the **Harlequin Reader Service:**
**IN U.S.A.:** P.O. Box 1341, Buffalo, NY 14240-8531
**IN CANADA:** P.O. Box 603, Fort Erie, Ontario L2A 5X3

**Want to try 2 free books from another series? Call 1-800-873-8635 or visit www.ReaderService.com.**

*Terms and prices subject to change without notice. Prices do not include sales taxes, which will be charged (if applicable) based on your state or country of residence. Canadian residents will be charged applicable taxes. Offer not valid in Quebec. This offer is limited to one order per household. Books received may not be as shown. Not valid for current subscribers to the Love Inspired or Love Inspired Suspense series. All orders subject to approval. Credit or debit balances in a customer's account(s) may be offset by any other outstanding balance owed by or to the customer. Please allow 4 to 6 weeks for delivery. Offer available while quantities last.

**Your Privacy**—Your information is being collected by Harlequin Enterprises ULC, operating as Harlequin Reader Service. For a complete summary of the information we collect, how we use this information and to whom it is disclosed, please visit our privacy notice located at corporate.harlequin.com/privacy-notice. From time to time we may also exchange your personal information with reputable third parties. If you wish to opt out of this sharing of your personal information, please visit readerservice.com/consumerschoice or call 1-800-873-8635. **Notice to California Residents**—Under California law, you have specific rights to control and access your data. For more information on these rights and how to exercise them, visit corporate.harlequin.com/california-privacy.

LIRLIS22R3

# HARLEQUIN PLUS

Try the best multimedia subscription service for romance readers like you!

---

## Read, Watch and Play.

Experience the easiest way to get the romance content you crave.

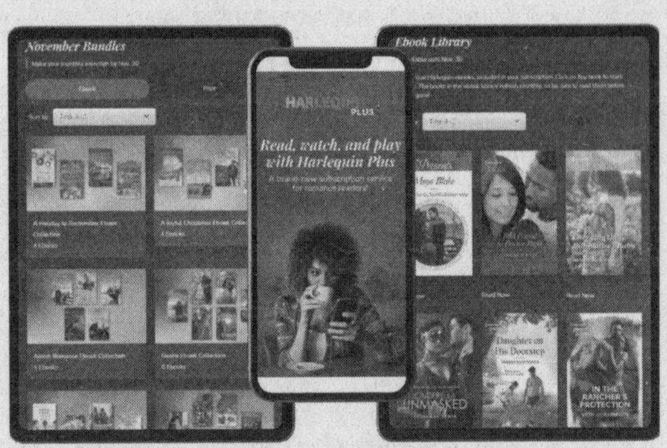


Start your **FREE TRIAL** at www.harlequinplus.com/freetrial.

HARPLUS0123